THE CAJUN WEREWOLF'S CAPTIVE

A STORMY WEATHER STORY

SELENA BLAKE

A Stormy Weather Story - Book 1
The Cajun Werewolf's Captive - Sebastian and Amanda

The Cajun Werewolf's Captive was previously titled The Cajun's Captive.

Payment of the download fee for this ebook grants the purchaser the non-exclusive, non-transferable right to download and read this file, and to maintain a private backup copy of the file for the purchaser's personal use ONLY.

Copyright ©2008, 2018 Selena Blake

All rights reserved.

This book is a work of fiction. Any resemblance to persons, living or dead, places or events is purely coincidental. Characters, events, and organizations within this work are products of the author's imagination and are used fictitiously.

ABOUT THE CAJUN WEREWOLF'S CAPTIVE

Billionaire werewolf Sebastian Deveraux needs a mate. According to his brothers, he's spent too much time in the spotlight. That's code for not putting the Pack first. They're right, but evenings with a starlet is easier than admitting the truth to himself.

He found his mate. And she'd run from him.

Amanda St. James is back in Louisiana for her father's funeral and not a moment longer. The place is steeped in memories, daydreams, and dangerous desires. It doesn't matter how smoking hot Sebastian is, she refuses to end up like her mother.

But Sebastian let his pride get in the way before. He's not going to make the same mistakes again. This time, he'll do whatever it takes to keep her.

Warning: Contains one sinfully seductive Cajun werewolf with plenty of pent up sexual tension, a little light bondage, and a love that will last a lifetime.

1

June

The low rumble of thunder drew Sebastian Deveraux's gaze to the East window. Just beyond the massive earthen wall was the dark, churning waters of the mighty Mississippi. The morning's slow drizzle turned into a downpour. He sighed, knowing that the hurricane looming in the Gulf of Mexico would wreak havoc with his shipping business, for the next few weeks at least.

The wet weather and dropping barometer made his joints ache. He knew he should at least call the office to make sure his second in command had things under control, but he was having a hard time convincing his body to get out of bed.

As the Alpha, it was his job to protect his pack and take care of their needs. And that took money. Before long, it would be time to sell Deveraux Shipping and fade into the woodwork.

Humans would get suspicious if the CEO of a shipping empire never seemed to age. Which was ironic considering how ancient he felt today. And lonely to boot.

In his wolf form, he rose up on all fours and stretched before heading to his closet. The original floors of the old plantation house were cool beneath his paws. He'd loved the wide pine planks on sight and hadn't wanted to do anything more than seal them and toss down a soft rug or two.

Inside his closet, he transformed into his human self, his muscles and bones stretching and compacting until he straightened to his full six feet four inches. He leaned his head to the right and heard, as much as felt, his neck pop. Today's muggy weather called for jeans and a T-shirt.

He was zipping his favorite pair of Levis when the scent of gumbo wafted under his nose. One of his brothers must be heating up last night's leftovers for breakfast. He sniffed the air appreciatively. Like any red-blooded man or beast, he loved to eat. Loved meat, loved anything that set his taste buds on fire and made his mouth water.

Dieu, he missed France. Missed the food, craved the bread, a sip of French wine straight from the vineyard. But he could never go back. He clenched his jaw at the flood of memories that rushed forth. It did no good to rehash that part of his past.

Slipping a T-shirt over his head, he strode to the kitchen and found André stirring the gumbo in a heavy cast iron pot. They nodded at each other in greeting.

"Coffee's on," André said, his deep voice sleepy and rough.

"*Merci.* Jules up yet?"

"*Non.* Think any more about what he said, *mon frère?*"

Sebastian had thought of little else. He hadn't gotten more than a few hours of sleep last night and those hours had been fraught with dreams of a life he was missing. Jules, and the rest of their small pack, wanted a secure future and everything that went with it. Mates, kids.

Sebastian wanted the same thing. But that security came with a price. As wealthy as he was, it didn't matter when he wasn't mated.

Being mated was a sign of security, one he longed to give his brothers and cousins. A complete Alpha pair. It would signify their future.

But when he thought of his other half, the woman who'd stand at his side, it wasn't a she-wolf he pictured. And when he thought of his pups, they didn't have dark hair like he and his brothers. They were angelic blonds with piercing blue eyes and infectious smiles.

Impossible. He mentally shook the thoughts away.

"I can't just pick up a mate at the market," Sebastian said. He'd said as much last night. And it's not like he'd ever find anyone who stirred his senses the way *she* had. There might be plenty of women with a quick wit and a sharp tongue that wouldn't let him get away with anything, but none of them would have her sparkling blue eyes and adorable laugh that sucker punched him every time.

André watched him with dark eyes. The same eyes that all the Deveraux men were blessed with: dark as night, filled with stormy emotions and a sense of cunning found only in a true predator.

"Forgive me, brother, but I don't think dating bimbos and celebrities is going to help in your search."

"I didn't realize I was searching," Sebastian said. He took a sip of the strong black elixir that promised to jolt him awake. The hot liquid hit his tongue and scalded its way down his throat.

Truth was, there was only one woman he'd ever wanted as a mate. But she obviously wasn't destined to be his other half, his *Luna*. She hadn't stuck around.

In fact, she'd run away.

The weight of his responsibility pressed down heavily on his shoulders. He knew he should step aside and let André become the Alpha, but nothing was that simple. There was no stepping aside for wolves. Everything had to be fought and won. And Sebastian had no intention of fighting his own brother.

After a long pause, André muttered, "You act like you're the only one she left behind. Like Jules and I didn't lo—"

Sebastian knew that all too well. "She was never yours to have," Sebastian clipped out, not ready to hear his brother confess his feelings.

André didn't look surprised or hurt at the outburst; he simply flicked his gaze to the floor, but Sebastian apologized anyway.

"You should go after her," his brother ventured.

Of course, he should. He should just trot up to New York, chase a woman who had disappeared from his life under the darkness of night.

"It wasn't meant to be."

André quirked up an eyebrow and stared him down over the rim of his coffee mug. Sebastian sometimes wondered if this mansion of a house was truly big enough for the five of them. His cousin Burke was the biggest of them all and sometimes he managed to dwarf what should have been sizable rooms. Burke's brother Laurent wasn't that much smaller, in height or breadth.

The refurbished kitchen was large, so large that there was easily eight feet of space between them and yet he could tell that his younger brother wanted to smack him upside the head.

And with André's training and reflexes, he could do it too.

"Are you still buying into that stars aligning crap? *Mon Dieu.*" André stepped toe to toe with him, his lips curling in a snarl. He looked every bit the killer he was trained to be: dark, intense, taut with tension and ready for battle. More likely, ready to knock some sense into Sebastian himself.

"Enough already, *mon frère*," André continued, his tone pleading. "If you want her, you must go get her."

He poked Sebastian in the chest and Sebastian let him. This had obviously been a long time in coming.

"Make her listen to reason. Find out why she ran. Bring her back and make her yours." André's voice rang with emotion. He almost sounded like he, himself, had been in love. Painfully, completely... and lost her.

"And how do you propose I do that?"

André took a step back. There was an elegant shrug to his wide shoulders.

"Tie her up if you have to."

The mention of tying her up sent fire through Sebastian's system. There was so much he needed to explain to her. But she wasn't likely to want to hear him, especially after all this time.

"There's one flaw with your plan. Have you

forgotten that she's human?"

André stared him down for another long moment before blinking. Then he turned to look out the window over the sink.

There was so much truth he needed to tell her, but she'd been so young. She was older now, yes, but the other half of the equation was still true. Could she handle it? Could he trust her? Maybe he should have trusted her all those years ago before the conflict and secrets had scared her away.

He stared at André for a long moment. "Maybe you're right." Swallowing his pride was tough, but the alternative was bleak. Pointless. He'd been living it for far too long.

"I know I am," André countered, not unkindly. "And she's worth it, whatever you have to do to get her back."

Sebastian nodded. He'd always known that. So why had he waited so long?

Before he could answer that question, a sharp sound outside caught his attention. Not thunder, nor rain. Something else. A low growl sounded from the hallway.

"Jules is up," Sebastian said and headed toward the sound. Even though he saw nothing out of place, he knew that the walls around his estate didn't keep out reporters, tourists, and the occasional woman, desperate for a wealthy husband. His sharper wolf senses took over as he slipped into his bedroom and looked around. It was just as he'd left it. He saw nothing but rain through the window, but his keen ears could hear someone breathing. He exited his room and moved toward the front of the house. His brother, Jules—still in furry form—was in the large foyer.

"You take the back," Sebastian told him and headed for the front door.

The wide porch wrapped all the way around the house and he quickly made his way to far side that ran the length of his bedroom. The rain beat on the roof above his head, drowning out his footsteps.

The blond peering into his bedroom window never heard him approach thanks to his bare feet and years of sneaking up on his prey. With her hands framing her eyes to block out the light, she didn't see him either.

"Can I help you?" he asked mildly when he was within pouncing distance.

Shrieking, she whirled to face him, backing up at the same time. Her hands dropped to balance herself, but it was too late. He made no move to rescue her even though he could have. Her momentum toppled her over the low railing. She landed flat on her back in the soggy grass below.

From the edge of the porch, he stared down at her not feeling the least bit sorry for startling her. What did a man have to do to get privacy?

Her wheat colored hair covered her face and

the rain slowly soaked her clothes. She seemed too startled to move. Finally, she eased up on her elbows. Her breasts heaved and fell as if she might start crying.

Mon Dieu. The last thing he wanted was a crying woman. Or a lawsuit.

"You all right?"

With a perfectly polished hand, she flicked her hair out of her face and glared up at him. The blue eyes that locked with his couldn't have surprised him more if there'd been eight of them.

Amanda St. James. Alive and in his yard.

Couldn't be. He narrowed his gaze and took in her features. Same cute pixie nose. Same rosy, heart-shaped mouth he'd longed to kiss. Same delicious curves that his hands itched to caress.

Suddenly he was transported a decade back in time when they'd all been hanging out on a hot summer day. It had been August. Suffocatingly humid. Amanda had grabbed the hose and proceeded to drench him and his brothers to the bone. Her kissable mouth had laughed and smiled as they'd chased her. When they'd finally caught her, turning the hose on her, the water had plastered her clothes to her sweet young body.

It had taken all his willpower not to carry her off that very afternoon. To kiss her all over—from that adorable nose, to those delicious berry pink lips, to her hot pink toenails.

The clap of thunder brought him back to the

present. His eyes didn't fool him. He sniffed the air and her scent filled his lungs. She smelled so sweet, so familiar, and so wonderful that he almost closed his eyes to savor it. Instead, he took in her pitiful form. She looked like a drowned cat. He watched as the rain molded her shirt to her breasts. Either from cold or, heaven help him, desire, her nipples beaded beneath the fabric and stood out like pebbles.

He clenched his fists. Long dormant need surged upward startling him with its intensity, its rawness. He hadn't seen or heard from her in nine long years, but he'd never stopped wanting her. It was the reason he dated a long stream of women, never settling down. He'd never felt this kind of urgency with anyone else.

Although he'd tried to wipe away her memory, none of them could compare to Manda. His Manda.

But her presence now reminded him of how she'd fled all those years ago. She'd gone off to Yankee country for school. Then she'd gone on to work for one of the biggest broadcast companies in the country. Never looked back. Never called. Simply fled. Ran from him.

His inner beast had been too proud to let him chase. Had been sure she'd come back in a week or two. Weeks had turned into years and now almost a decade. The beast growled deep inside, for the years he'd lost, for making him want her so, making him wait. It lay coiled, anxious and ready to spring to life and take what it wanted.

He crossed his arms over his chest, trying to keep the dangerous animal inside on a tight leash.

"Well, well, well. If it isn't Amanda St. James." He couldn't keep the disdain from his voice. He hoped to hell she couldn't hear the hurt, the yearning... "Did the Yanks kick you out? Get too cold for ya up north?"

"What a mean thing to say." For a moment, she looked genuinely wounded. But he told himself that was part of her game. The network probably sent her. How he didn't want that to be true…

"Then what are ya doin' here?" Probably snooping for a story, he thought. *Figured she'd use her looks, her connections, to get it. Like hell, she was going to get her story.*

Her tongue slipped between her glossy pink lips to lick a raindrop. That simple movement reminded him of all the times she'd licked her lips, stuck out her tongue at him—reminded him of everything he really wanted in life.

And just how much he wanted to kiss her.

Once again, he took in her sad wet form and saw everything he'd wanted for hundreds of years. Everything he'd been denied and had denied himself.

Sebastian knew he couldn't be angry; she was worth the wait. And regardless of why she was suddenly back in his life, he couldn't let her get away again. This was a sign from the gods. She was meant to be his. He'd known it all those years ago when he'd watched her blossom in front of his eyes. While he'd waited for her to grow up, waited for her to come to him.

He still knew it. Nothing had changed, he reasoned. Except that he wanted her more now than he had nine years ago.

And she was well over eighteen now. He would finally make her his.

With the effortless grace his kind was known for, he leapt over the railing and landed at her feet. Oblivious to the rain, he glared down at her.

"Up," he ordered, offering her his hand. He was prepared for the bolt of electricity that would travel through him the instant her skin touched his. That awareness had always affected him, also reminded him that she was something special.

Rather than take his hand, she started to crab crawl backwards, but she couldn't get away fast enough. In a lightning fast move, he threw her over his shoulder. She barely weighed more than a sack or two of sugar.

"What are you doing?" she cried.

"Taking what's mine."

He knew the instant she comprehended his words. She wiggled like a bunny in a trap, but it didn't matter. He had her where he wanted her.

For now.

2

"Put me down!"

"Relax, *chérie.*" He carried her around to the front of the house and across the threshold, past the open wooden door. His brothers were nowhere to be seen.

"I'll give you the quick tour," he said, knowing she couldn't see more than the floor. "The foyer. This is the hallway. And this..." He deposited her in the middle of his oversized bathroom. "Is the bathroom."

He took in her wet, lush form. Her nipples were still beaded beneath the fabric and she crossed her arms over her chest and gave him a pointed look. He raised an eyebrow; she shouldn't be surprised. From the first moment he'd seen her sitting on her porch railing, he'd loved what he saw.

Sebastian would be forever grateful for the

mundane detour that had brought her into his life. If the old bridge on the way to their house hadn't been broken and in need of repairs, he wouldn't have taken the backroad where Amanda's house was. He had no need to drive past the small, well worn row of homes. It wasn't a short cut. But the bridge had been out, he had steered his truck onto her street and she'd been sitting there on her porch, drawing him like a moth to a flame.

"Who do you think you are?" As if the chill had worn off, her eyes blazed up at him and color stained her cheeks even as droplets of water slid down her creamy skin.

She'd always been the embodiment of beauty. Natural, wholesome, dazzling in her sweetness. Even now, in her black Capris and soaking white top that would give any woman in a wet T-shirt contest a run for her money. Even when she looked angry as fire, there was still a sweetness about her.

Why was *she* angry? She'd left *him*. And now, she was the one trespassing on his property. It wasn't his fault she'd done a back flip into the mud. Okay, so technically it was his fault since he'd surprised her, but…

"You know exactly who I am, *chérie*. Or have you forgotten since you ran away?"

"I have no idea what you're talking about."

He could tell she was trying not to shiver, not

show him any weakness. His wolf appreciated her courage even as her eyes feigned innocence.

"Don't play innocent, doll. You know who I am, just like I know who you are. I've always known."

"You're right. I know what you are. What I want to know is why you're acting like a caveman!"

"What is it you think you know, *petite*?" he asked, ignoring her last question.

She backed away from him, her eyes going wide. "*Loup-garou*," she whispered, her bottom lip trembling.

Her French was surprisingly rusty, and he threw back his head and laughed. "You think I'm a Cajun werewolf? That I kill bad little Catholics? Is that what you think?"

"I saw you."

Shit. Had she been watching when he'd walked into his closet? Perhaps it was time to call his decorator to install some automatic blinds.

"Hey, Wolf. Come!" he called to his brother. A few moments later, Jules, still in his wolf form, padded into the bathroom. Sebastian could see the surprise, the interest in his brother's keen brown eyes. His rough brown coat seemed to bristle when he looked up at Amanda.

"Is this what you saw?" he asked her.

"It's a trick!" Her hands came down on her hips and she scowled at them.

"No trick, *chérie*. Now, why don't you tell me what you're really doing here?" He bent down and scratched Jules behind the ears as he would a dog. Jules hated this kind of treatment, but Sebastian knew he was accepting it because he wanted to know why lil' Manda St. James was in Sebastian's bathroom.

"I—I didn't know this was your house." She was lying through her pretty pink lips. Jules must have known it, too, because he growled low in his throat. Manda backed up another step and hit the granite counter top. She reached back to steady herself.

"S'okay boy," he reassured quietly and glanced back up at her. "We don't believe that *chérie*. We know you're here to do a story on me. What's your angle? Big businessman dating Hollywood Starlet? Or are you going for something more local?"

"I don't know what you're talking about," she repeated. This time her voice didn't quiver. She actually sounded like she believed what she was saying.

"Really? Go get something to eat, Wolf," he said, dismissing his brother. Jules slowly backed from the room and trotted away. Sebastian straightened and stepped toward her until they were toe-to-toe.

She leaned away with a little gasp that told him she wasn't as calm as she wanted him to believe. There was desire in the depths of those pretty blue eyes and her body called to his. He longed to pinch her nipples between his fingers until she cried out his name. Until she begged him to take her.

Instead, he settled for placing a hand on the counter on either side of her and leaning in close. This way he wouldn't miss a detail of her reaction.

"I know about you too," he continued. "How you ran away. Went to Columbia. Graduated with honors. Went on to sign with ABC. You just got promoted. What am I missing, Amanda?"

"I didn't run away," she told him firmly, even as she shivered.

"I don't believe you, but it doesn't matter. This is a game you don't want to play with me. I might have lost you all those years ago, but I'm not going to lose this time. You're back and I don't intend to let you leave again."

He didn't give her a chance to say a word. Instead, he flicked the shower on and gave her a dark look that told her to do exactly what he said.

"Get out of those wet clothes."

The way her mouth dropped open in shock would have amused him had she not then glanced at the door as if to gauge how quickly she could get away from him.

"So, you don't catch cold. You're welcome to use my shower to warm up, *chérie*," he said, letting his voice drop to a seductive low. Then he turned to leave. "But I can't promise I won't join you," he said from the doorway.

Sebastian closed the door behind Jules and himself and heard her yell after him.

"You're a rat, Sebastian Deveraux."

3

Trembling, Amanda sank down onto the cold tile floor. She stared at the door Sebastian had just exited and wondered what she'd gotten herself into. He wasn't the same man she remembered. Gorgeous with a sensuality that should have been illegal, yes, but he was also angry. And if she could trust his words, possessive.

He'd looked so predatory. Like the animal she'd always thought him to be. So much the same and yet different. Harder.

Tall, dark, dangerously handsome. Deep brown eyes, jet black hair, and a tan from years in the sunny South. The small scar on his jaw added to his dangerous sex appeal.

She remembered the first time she'd ever seen him with crystal clear clarity. It'd been hot as hell that August afternoon. Her mother had just moved them into a one-bedroom shanty a stone's throw from the swamp. The yard had been a pitiful mix of dust and dried up chicken bones.

At sixteen she'd been counting down the days until she turned eighteen and could move out on her own. Legally move out anyway, not that momma would have cared much. One less mouth of feed and all that.

With her t-shirt tied between her breasts, what little there was of them, to beat the heat, she stretched out on the rickety porch railing, glad to have a handful of shade to call her own. With a wrinkled second-hand copy of Cosmo on her lap, she fanned herself with an envelope. There was probably a bill or an eviction notice (there was always an eviction notice) inside but she didn't look. She didn't care.

Momma had moved them, again. There'd be a new school and no friends in her future. The reason why they'd moved to the middle of nowhere, again, no longer mattered.

The only thing that mattered in her world was moving out on her own, getting to a bigger city and making something of herself. She applied herself in school and knew that she might be eligible for scholarships.

The magazine made womanhood seem glamorous. She yearned for a solid career and a steady relationship with someone who wasn't named Bubba. But more than that really, the articles and pictures made life seem fun again, adventurous.

The sense of control and empowerment spoke to her like nothing in the bayou did.

A car door slammed, and her head popped up, daydream burst. The envelope in her hand froze in mid-air as she locked gazes with a dark-haired man. The breath stalled in her throat as she took in his tall, lean frame. Wide shoulders and just the right amount of muscle on display beneath the black polo shirt. There wasn't a hint of flab on him which set him apart in a world of fishermen who had *dunlap* disease.

Who was he? And why did she feel like those dark eyes took in all of her with a single glance?

Two more just like him exited the shiny truck. They had to be brothers; they were blessed with the same inky dark hair and sinful good looks.

The three of them were certainly not what she'd expected when her mother had dumped their belongings in the tiny bedroom this morning. The little house next door was a bit larger than their rental, not that that was saying much.

But the porch and yard were tidy. This close to the bayou she'd expected a redneck in a wife-beater. She'd been around long enough to know that sometimes the stereotype fit like a glove and this shitty little burg so far out of town, well, the shoe fit.

The truck looked brand new and no one she knew had that kind of cash. They strode across the dirt yard and onto the sparsely decorated porch. Surely, they weren't her new neighbors. If they could afford a truck like that…

The last one, he looked the youngest, nodded at her.

She lifted her hand in a wave and felt a fresh wave of heat crash over her.

They couldn't be all that much older than her.

Amanda tipped her head against the cool bathroom cabinet and let her mind drift back from that fateful summer day.

After everything she'd seen this morning, the wolf, the possessiveness in Sebastian, a little voice whispered for her to run. But she'd run before and where had it gotten her?

No answers. And though fear trickled down her spine at the uncertainty, she was tempted to find out the truth. All those years ago she'd thought him too handsome, with an animal magnetism that couldn't be denied.

She was Louisiana born and bred and she had a healthy sense of superstition. Her brain was shocked, her heart, not so much. How was it possible? Were her eyes playing tricks on her?

Or perhaps Sebastian was playing with her. A secret like that…sure the locals would shrug it off. But the media? The rest of the world? They'd go after him like big foot or the Loch Ness monster.

Her stomach cramped at the implications. Did she really want to know the truth? Would he let her go after seeing what she'd seen?

A decade ago she'd had a painful crush on him. On all of them, really. They might have lived in the swamp but there was an urbaneness, a gentlemanly quality in them that belied their years.

AND THOUGH SHE'D flirted with all of them just as they'd flirted with her, she'd never let on just how deep her feelings for Sebastian went. When he wasn't treating her like a kid sister, he'd looked at her like she was the only woman he'd ever wanted. And that was the rub, he'd made her feel grown up, smart, beautiful, not at all like what she really was. A young, confused, poor girl growing up in the wilds of Louisiana who was barely out of a training bra.

Luckily that'd changed before she'd hit eighteen, but her growth spurt had only fueled the heat in their eyes. And that was about the time that the tension between the brothers had started to get to her.

Sebastian had played hot and cold so often she'd felt like her head was spinning.

Three days after graduation she'd moved away. Away from his reach, the temptation. Terrified of the rift growing between the three men, she'd packed her bags and hopped the first bus out of town. Away from what she'd always known would be her destruction: love for a man who didn't love her the way she loved him.

Gosh, that seemed like an eternity ago.

She'd thrown herself into school and then into work. All the while, telling herself that she could get over him, that she *was* over him.

And then she'd received that note.

God help her, she'd convinced herself that there wouldn't be anything between them. No more chemistry, no more mushy insides when he smiled at her just so, no more aching in her heart when he showed off that protective side of his nature that she'd always loved.

But he was more potent now than he'd ever been.

What the hell had she been thinking, coming here?

She hadn't been thinking. Not really. Just following her heart. Her heart that had stupidly been seduced by a gorgeous arrangement of flowers and a few words on a crisp linen card.

She massaged her temples trying to ward off the impending headache. It didn't help. She shivered, more from desire than the cold. Her skin was chilled and clammy though.

Steam rose above the glass doors of the shower, beckoning to her. Slowly, she stood up. How was it after all this time he knew her so well? Why did a single glance from him make her knees quake? Was it the smooth way he'd jumped over the railing that sent her heart racing or perhaps it was the predatory way he'd stalked toward her. Hell, it was probably sheer closeness, the masculine scent of him and the dreamy accent that made her blood pressure soar.

He'd seemed positively shocked to find her on his property, she mused as she stripped out of her clothes. Angry about it. But surely, he expected to hear from her?

She blew out a sigh and glanced at the sleek white marble vanity. He'd had the whole house redone. She remembered the property from before, back when it'd been his dream to restore the home to its former glory. Did Andre and Jules live here too? Had Burke and Laurent moved in like he'd planned?

"Finally using a little of your money, Sebastian?" she whispered to the empty room.

She'd daydreamed about creating a home with him. At the time she'd been as enamored with the idea of having her own bedroom as sharing it with him. And if she'd had to pick the finishes, this room would have been it.

Maybe she was dreaming…all of it. This perfect room, the delicious male who aroused as easily as he infuriated. She pinched herself. *Ouch.* Definitely awake. Still in Sebastian Deveraux's enormous bathroom. Still shivering from cold and desire.

He'd leaned close, too close for comfort, and

stared into her eyes as if he could read all her secrets.

She bit her lip, knowing he probably could. She stepped into the large tile shower and let the hot water rain down on her skin, driving away the cold. It made her want to moan with delight, but she didn't dare.

She reached for the bottle of shampoo and inhaled the refreshing scent of juniper and eucalyptus. It did little to calm the rapid pulse in her veins.

Even after all this time, he could still make her tremble. She still yearned for his touch, was dying for his kiss; still craved the completion she'd secretly known that only he could bring.

But the things she'd heard about him and his brothers were true. Softly spoken words carried on the winds. She'd known it. The reality of what she'd seen hadn't surprised her, but it made her tremble. She'd always had a gut feeling about the handsome Deveraux men and she always listened to her gut.

Except for when it had told her to stay in Louisiana all those years ago. To fight for him.

She couldn't end up like her mother. She wouldn't.

And right now, her gut was telling her to get as far away from Sebastian as possible. Before she did something crazy, like beg him to make love to her.

. . .

Sebastian rewound the security recording half an hour and watched as a compact car pulled up just outside the east wall and stopped. Amanda alighted from the car and stared at the heavy wrought iron gate.

A frown marred her beautiful face as she stepped toward the driveway. Even from the distance the cameras had caught her curious glances. She seemed to take in the high brick walls, the paved drive and the lush magnolias lining the drive before reaching for the call button. But she hesitated.

Sebastian leaned forward. Why was she hesitating? *Push the button, chérie.*

She pulled her hand back and looked up at the house again. He switched to the camera hidden on the front porch. There at the end of the long straight driveway he saw her slender frame behind the thick black bars of the gate. She turned away. But no sooner had she disappeared from view she stalked back across the driveway.

Her shoulders were down, and her chin was up.

Once again, she stared up the driveway and the house, her gaze all but connecting with the camera lens. Did she have any idea she was being taped? What was going through that pretty head of hers? And why did seeing her on a video recording make places inside him melt and rejoice at having her so close again.

A handful of seconds ticked by and she disappeared again. He scanned the other camera angles and saw her head pop over the wall on the left side of the gate. Mouth screwed up in exertion, she pushed up and straddled the top. Her chest heaved as she caught her breath and then hopped to the ground on the inside of the compound.

He had to give it to her. She was a determined and agile woman. Her fellow journalists would be proud.

He watched her stride toward the house, his gut tightening with each step she took. It was a silly reaction of course; she was already a wall away in his bathroom. Very likely naked in his shower. *Dieu* help him. He could be naked in there with her.

His attention zipped back to the video before him. After a tentative step on the bottom stair, she glanced around and then hurried up the stairs. She paused for a moment and seemed to be collecting herself. If she was here for an interview, why was she slinking around? And why did she seem to be scared of getting caught?

She didn't have a camera bag, recorder or notebook in hand. He didn't believe her story of course, but she didn't seem to be on an official mission for her station. Wouldn't she have arrived with a camera man?

She glanced up at the ceiling and then paused as she turned to look back at the manicured lawn.

The way she paused and leaned against the railing stole his breath and transported him back in time. She'd needed to visit a local plantation to write a school paper and her mother was gone on one of her benders. Why the woman didn't accept that the bastard was never going to change for her, never going to stop sleeping around, never going to settle down with her… She was too nice to see what was written so plainly in front of her face.

Everyone had their faults. Sebastian had offered to take Amanda to the plantation before his brothers or cousins got home. He couldn't chance her getting a ride from one of them. But a quick field trip had turned into so much more. He'd become absorbed by her, enthralled with the rhythm of her heartbeat to the soft sound of her breathing.

They'd explored for what seemed like hours. She'd blown him away with her witty responses and knowledge, her drive to break the cycle and get a good job. Her desire to build a career brought a smile to his lips and she'd turned toward him with those soulful blue eyes and grinned back.

"What?"

"You should do that more often," she replied.

"Do what?"

"Smile," she said simply and continued toward a massive magnolia.

Dozens of creamy, lemon scented magnolia blossoms had nothing on Amanda's own heady fragrance. He'd followed her, eager to soak in every second.

"I guess I don't have much to smile about," he murmured, watching her closely. As long as he lived he would never forget the sight of her, so young and achingly beautiful, stretching up to sniff one of the massive blooms. Her fingers grazed the soft petals and he'd been instantly jealous. Hard as a rock, wanting her touch more than he wanted his next breath. She was intoxicating.

"You're such a liar, Sebastian," she said, turning his face toward him. A grin tugged the corner of her lips and he felt his heart contract. So that was it. She was *it*, the one he'd always waited for. After decades of searching, he'd found her, his mate, in his own back yard.

If only she wasn't so fucking young.

And innocent. *Dieu*. Completely innocent, not to mention human.

He bit back a curse and settled for a long sigh.

She was really something, calling him on his bullshit.

"How do you figure that, *chérie*?"

He really needed to stop with the endearments. She was too young, too inexperienced and he was too old, too hard, too rough for a beauty like her. Maybe when she was older…

"You have a family who loves you therefore you have plenty of reasons to smile."

She stepped away the moment the words left her lips and his heart broke for her. Cracked and splintered right there in his chest cavity. Though he knew her mother loved her, he also knew that her mother loved her father more. Much more.

According to Manda her parents had a volatile on again-off again relationship. And unfortunately, Manda was never going to stack up against the possibility of being with the man who'd donated his sperm all those years ago.

Sebastian wondered, not for the first time, if he shouldn't step in and solve their problem for them. But he was also a believer in letting fate run its course.

He followed her up onto the wide porch, eager to sooth her pain. He could feel the sadness coming off her in waves. Just as he was about to reach out she'd tripped on a warped board and tumbled backward into his arms.

His reflexes had saved her from falling and possible injury, but they'd also brought her body into direct contact with his. In the circle of his arms she'd tipped her chin up and uttered a breathless thank you. He'd seen the awareness in her eyes, felt it in the way her body submitted to his. Heaven help him he'd wanted, no needed, to kiss her so badly.

If the guide hadn't peeked around the corner to tell them the grounds were closing, he would have slanted his lips across hers and taken everything she'd been offering. Her sweetness, her pleasure, her innocence.

Back in the here and now he watched himself leap over the railing after her and quickly rewound the recording to the point where he'd gotten lost in thought.

She'd turned back from the yard, glanced at window before taking in the wide floorboards. Nibbling her lower lip, he could almost see the memory running through her mind. It was the conversation they'd had there on the porch at that old plantation where he'd assured her she could have anything her heart desired. Anything at all and his heart had been shouting 'pick me!'

She'd smiled at him and told him she wanted a home of her own with a big front porch and lots of magnolias. A place where she could have lots of friends and family congregate and when the world intruded she could wander into the garden and pick her own magnolia flowers.

The picture she'd painted that day was vivid and had stuck with him as he'd had this house renovated. He'd included everything she'd ever wanted without even realizing it. The big porch, dozens of magnolias, a kitchen large enough to hold a whole crazy pack and then some.

Hell. He had to get to the bottom of this before his heart ran away with him again. He'd lost her once and he sincerely didn't want to repeat the experience.

He glanced at his watch as he strode from his study. He paused outside the bathroom door. Exactly thirty minutes before, he'd deposited her in the bathroom and he was tired of waiting around. He didn't bother to knock. It was, after all, his bathroom and she was the trespasser. She squeaked in surprise and tightened the fluffy white towel around her wet body.

"Privacy please!"

He dropped his gaze to the pile of clothes heaped on the floor. Knowing that the lacy bra and barely-there thong had been hugging her sweet body most of the day only fueled the flames inside him.

"I thought you said I was da Big Bad Wolf, *chérie*. Now you call me a rat. Yes, I heard you," he said when she raised her eyebrows. "Any other animals I remind you of?"

Her chin came up and she stared at him with crystal blue eyes. Her hair hung over her shoulder like honey colored waterfalls.

"*Non? Bien.* Gumbo's ready." He made for the door, scooping up her clothes and sandals as he went.

"Sebastian!"

"What is it, *petite*?"

"Clothes?"

"Ahh. I thought you might come to the table in da nude?"

"You're out of your mind," she told him hotly. Her fire fed his, but she didn't know that.

"You won't always think dat. I assure you. There's a robe inside dat door." He turned on the Cajun accent and charm because he knew she wouldn't be able to resist. You could take a girl out of da swamp, but you couldn't stop her from lovin' a Cajun.

"Thank you."

―――

JULES WAS TRANSFORMED, dressed and sitting at the old pine table in the kitchen by the time Sebastian finished tossing Manda's clothes in the washer. If he had his say, she wouldn't be needing them for quite some time.

Delicious aromas wafted from the stove: sausage and shrimp, rice and beans, and several spices. His stomach growled.

"What the hell's she doin' here?" Jules asked, curiosity and concern lacing his words. His hands clamped around a mug as André poured them all a fresh cup of coffee. There was electricity in the air that had nothing to do with the storm outside and everything to do with the woman under their roof.

Years ago, they'd fought over her. Fought like the wolves they were. And in the end, none of them had won her. If everything went according to his plan, as quickly devised as it was, they'd have their Luna, and he'd have his mate.

"Not sure yet. Probably snoopin' for a story," Sebastian said.

"I doubt it," André murmured.

Jules' brows furrowed. "You've got that look," he said.

André nodded.

"What look?" Sebastian stirred the gumbo.

"The 'yer up to something' look."

"Yer right. I'm cookin'."

Jules just laughed and added another spoon to the table.

"How's the hurricane?" Sebastian asked.

"Cat 2. The dry air'll slow down winds. It's comin' quick though."

Sebastian agreed with that. Third storm of the season and it was moving fast. Wind speed didn't concern him as much as the water, but there was a good chance it would pass them by.

"Laurent called. They've got things handled at the docks. Just in case."

Thank goodness for his cousins.

He heard the gentle footfalls before Manda poked her head around the corner. Her blonde hair was still damp and stringy. She paused at the sight of them and he knew she was trying to decide if she should have made a run for it. The uncertainty in her gaze almost killed him.

Surely, she knew he'd never hurt her, he'd die before he let anyone else hurt her. She might have disappeared from his life, but he'd kept a close watch over her from afar.

"Welcome home stranger," Jules said, breaking the ice. She gave him a tight-lipped smile and then nodded to André before settling her gaze on Sebastian.

Seeming to steal her spine, she stepped into the room, bringing a scent of freshness with her. This house had never known a feminine hand and everything in him liked how adorable she looked standing barefoot in his kitchen.

Snatching her gaze from his, leaving him bereft, she glanced back at his brothers.

"Hi Jules, André. It's good to see you."

Jules looked her up and down with an appreciative glint in his eye. "You too."

What André had said about them all wanting her was true. Was true even now. Sebastian could smell their blood pumping through their veins.

Her skin was free from the mud and grass, fresh and clean. She looked small and fragile in Sebastian's big black robe. In fact, it looked like she'd had to wrap it around herself twice.

He smiled. The knowledge that she was naked

beneath the robe made parts of him stir. He couldn't help letting his gaze fall on the large wooden table between them, knowing it would easily support their weight. That he could push open the robe and feast his eyes on her body, trail his hands over her flesh, sink into her until they were both complete.

"Um, do you have a first aid kit?"

Her words pulled him from his lust-filled fantasy. She held out her hand, palm up. He saw a faint scratch. Irritated with himself for scaring her and making her fall, he crossed the room and took her hand in his.

"I couldn't find one and—"

He felt her heartbeat race beneath his touch and a flash of sensation shot up his fingers, across his palm, and up his arm.

"I'll get it," Jules volunteered.

Her silky-smooth skin was cool, soft. It took all his control not to kiss her wrist. The beast inside demanded he trail his tongue along the delicate vein coursing just below her skin. Would she let him, or would she snatch her hand back?

Didn't matter. He enjoyed a good chase. He was, after all, a wolf in human clothing.

"Here ya go." Jules handed him the first aid kit. Who knew how old this thing was. Actually, that was a lie. He'd purchased it eleven years ago when he'd hoped that she would move in.

Sebastian gently directed Manda to a nearby

chair and opened the white metal box. With a few swift movements, he applied a bandage, inwardly chanting to himself that soon she would be his.

"Something smells good," she said and pulled her hand from his grasp.

She smelled good. Good enough to lick, nibble, and taste. He'd always thought she smelled of raspberries, but right now, she smelled fresh, like rain and his body wash. He liked the way his scent clung to her skin, marking her.

Sebastian glanced at Jules. His eyes were stormy gray. Undoubtedly, he could smell her freshness too.

"Let me serve it up, then," Sebastian said quickly. He could feel Manda looking at him as he pulled the bowls off the shelf and began ladling out the gumbo. What was she thinking? Was she regretting her decision to trespass? Did she buy his deception that Jules had been the wolf she'd seen? Could he tell her the truth? Would she believe him? Would she run? He couldn't chance it.

"So, Sebastian says you're here to do a story on him," Jules said, cocking his head to the side as he regarded her. Sebastian sat a bowl on the table in front of each of them and then stood back to watch.

"He misunderstood. I'm not here to do a story on him. I wouldn't do that."

"Really?" Jules glanced at Sebastian before pegging her with another stare.

"Even after he broke up with Carmen what's-her-name?"

"Not even after he broke up with Carmen what's-her-name," she said flatly and dipped into the gumbo.

"We went out once," Sebastian grumbled. Paparazzi were such monsters. He never should have gone out with the woman.

"He's still the most eligible bachelor in Louisiana, you know."

Jules would have made a great lawyer, Sebastian thought. He wasn't giving away anything that wasn't public knowledge or opinion, but he was definitely turning up the heat under Manda. He stifled a grin as she shifted uncomfortably in her seat.

"Course, you probably knew that. Working at the Network and all. Bet it's easy to keep tabs on old *friends*." He stretched out the last word.

"What do you want me to say? I told you I'm not here to do a story on him."

"Are you here to do a story on me?" Jules asked. He wiggled his eyebrows and gave her that almost canine smile Sebastian knew most women found charming. He wasn't pleased to see her frown turn into the slightest of smiles.

"Why would I do a story on you?" she asked.

Jules leaned across the table, his polo shirt outlining his muscular build.

"Because, *chérie*. I'm the second most eligible bachelor in Louisiana."

The wolf inside demanded Sebastian claim her as his and right now, but he mentally tightened the leash. He didn't want to scare her. He wanted her screaming with pleasure, not fear.

Jules was just having fun, flirting as usual, but Sebastian didn't like it. André didn't either if the thunderous look on his face was any indication.

Sebastian needed space. And some time. They needed to discuss a few things and he needed to get her far away from civilization for what he had in mind.

"Sorry. I'm not here for you," she told him. She tried to regain her composure, control of the situation and at the very least, her emotions. But Jules' smile dazzled her, made her long for the old days. Her tongue tangled, and the words came out wrong. She didn't mean to imply that she was here for Sebastian…

He stood close by, hovering with a bowl in his hands, his presence unnerving, and Jules looked as if he wanted to eat her. He was just as breathstealingly handsome as his brothers. Jet-black hair that glistened in the overhead light…piercing eyes so dark she could be staring into the night sky...tanned skin stretched over hard muscles. It was enough to make a girl drool.

With her hand tended to, she focused on the food in front of her. She forced down a spoon full of gumbo. The flavors exploded on her tongue. It was better than anything she'd ever tasted in New York and made her miss the locals here in Louisiana. The heat and texture combined to do a little Cajun dance in her mouth and she wanted to groan, but she wasn't about to give Sebastian the satisfaction.

So, the man could cook. Big deal. Why couldn't she have found a man in New York who could cook? Weren't there a billion chefs in New York City?

"So, you're here for him?" Jules asked not missing a beat.

She forced herself to meet his gaze. "Ever thought about a career in journalism? You've got the interrogation part down pat."

"Somehow, I don't think that was a compliment."

"It wasn't."

"Why are you here?" Sebastian asked. His voice was deep, heavenly.

Amanda looked at him and her breath faltered. He was leaning against the counter, his legs crossed at the ankles, long nimble fingers hugging the bowl.

Was he really so clueless? It didn't matter. She

just needed to get out of here pronto and figure out what she was going to do with herself for the rest of her life, now that she knew time and distance wouldn't change her feelings for this man. As possessive as he was, as attractive as he was, she refused to stay with a man who didn't love her.

It was safer to be alone than to slowly wither away, devoting herself to someone who didn't love her back. It'd taken courage to walk away the first time. She'd find it again…no matter how curious she was.

He stepped forward, gazing down at her with probing eyes. The moment reminded her so much of the day her mother had died that she was instantly transported back to the tiny kitchen. André'd been sitting on one side of the small square table, a cup of coffee in front of him. Jules had been standing by the sink.

Hot, fat tears rolled down her cheeks. She couldn't stop them. Didn't want to. She remembered the heat, the pain, the emptiness like it was yesterday.

"Where's Sebastian?" she asked in a broken voice, the syllables broken to the point where she wasn't sure the men had understood her. But Jules had immediately stepped forward and wrapped his arms around her. It wasn't his comfort she'd been seeking, and he seemed to instinctively know that she'd made her decision.

They'd never asked her to choose between them. But she had. In her heart it'd always been Sebastian.

"What happened, petite?" André asked softly as Jules deposited her into an empty chair.

She sat so she didn't fall. Her mom was gone. They'd come to the school and picked her up, driven her home. The car was totaled, whatever that meant. She figured it meant she had no way to get around.

THE FRONT DOOR BANGED SHUT. "André—where is she?"

Sebastian's voice filled the house as he sped into the room. His gaze locked on her and he stopped, then reached for her. She was already out of her chair, stepping into his arms. He held her close as she cried. No words, just quiet, steady warm comfort. Sebastian. Her rock.

For a moment she felt like everything would be okay. Sebastian made her feel invincible, immortal, loved. His hand rubbed up and down her back soothingly. She sobbed against his shirt, but he didn't utter a complaint, simply murmured into her hair. The words were French, soft and sweet and though she didn't understand them, she knew what he was telling her.

Her breath caught when he said the two words she'd been longing to hear for well over a year. Mon amour. My love.

She looked up into his face, seeking the truth. Was it simply another casual, careless endearment tossed out at random or did he mean it? She'd never know Sebastian to say what he didn't mean

He cupped her cheeks and stared at her lips. The heat

in his eyes was rivaled only by the electricity in the air. A thick current of tension surrounded them and she remembered that they weren't alone. But that knowledge didn't stop the desire swirling inside her. Her tears dried, and the hiccups stopped. She needed to feel his lips against hers. She'd know the truth then.

He ducked his head until their lips were an inch away, eyes locked with hers as if seeking permission. He had it. He'd always had it. Needn't ask.

Heat flushed through her and she felt a little light headed. Pure animal magnetism. That's how her mother had described the connection with her father. Amanda finally got it, finally understood why her mom had waited around for a man who couldn't commit to her, who didn't love her heart and soul above all others. But her mother had been so sure that her love was enough, that one day he'd wake up and see the family he was missing. He would never see them now. She was gone. Her soul wrapped around an old oak tree far more stubborn than she.

"Bastian," André's voice warned softly.

A sound rumbled from Sebastian's chest that was so low and so lethal that Amanda took a step back. That faltering step brought her up against another hard male body. André, she guessed, since Jules was standing off in the corner glowering at them.

"Manda," Sebastian murmured but his voice was deeper, rougher than she'd ever heard before. Almost like he was…growling.

The growling made sense now that she knew what he was. And just like all those years ago, a little voice in the back of her mind told her to run. She'd always erred on the side of flight rather than fight. And perhaps that meant she didn't always get what she really wanted, but self-preservation was important to. At least it had been that day.

Proverbial tail tucked between her legs, she'd sped out their backdoor into the balmy evening.

Today there was nowhere to run and nowhere to hide. He had her clothes and her keys were somewhere in the mud underneath a downpour. A clap of thunder made her jump and she saw Sebastian's keen eyes track the movement. As always, he saw too much.

She found it hard to formulate an excuse and decided the truth was her best bet.

"I got the flowers. Thank you," she said and turned back to her own bowl. Chill bumps broke out over her skin as they always did when Sebastian was near. Her nipples began to harden into little peaks. She couldn't help staring at his fingers, wondering what they would feel like on her skin.

"Flowers?" Jules and Sebastian echoed in unison.

She nodded. "At my father's funeral. They were beautiful."

"Funeral?" Sebastian asked. He sounded puzzled.

Unease settled over her and she frowned up at him.

"Yes, *Sebastian*." She emphasized his name. "The flowers you sent. Last week, after my father died."

"You sent her flowers?" André asked, looking pleased.

"I have the note in my car. I thought—" she broke off. Oh, it didn't matter what she thought. Obviously, she'd been wrong. Again. Just like she had all those years ago. Only last time, she'd had the proof of how foolish her thoughts were from his own mouth.

His secretary had probably sent the stupid flowers, but that didn't explain how he hadn't known about the funeral.

He knelt in front of her. "What did you think?" he asked, his tone quiet and seductive.

She glanced over at Jules and then André. He was crazy if he thought she was going to offer a confession. Especially in front of his brothers—

"Leave us," he bit out.

She jumped at the terse tone and stared, wide-eyed, after Jules and André as they walked out of the room, gumbo in hand.

She fumed. So, he was still playing games, confusing her. Playing the alpha dog and driving a wedge.

"You should be nicer to them," she said.

"They understand that we need our space."

"Oh yeah?"

"*Oui.* Now tell me. What did you think when you got this letter?"

"You know what? It doesn't matter. I really need to go. I have a plane to catch. Are my clothes ready?"

"They're in the wash." He gripped the arms of her chair. "And you're not going anywhere."

His tone had changed to one full of authority, only adding to her rising irritation. The perfect example of hot and cold. He'd been so sweet, so tender two minutes ago and now he was acting like a cave man again.

Why the hell had she even come back here? She could have just sent a thank you card. Honestly, what had she expected? Him to throw open his front door, get down on his knees and profess his undying love for her? Admit his stupidity at letting her go in the first place, and then for not coming after her for nine years?

Hah. Like that was going to happen.

Gathering her wits, she shoved the chair back and stood.

"You know what Sebastian—"

"What?" He was toe-to-toe with her, crowding her. She took a step back, but he followed, a predatory gleam in his eyes.

She swallowed. No. Her eyes weren't playing tricks on her. There was a danger in him—

His cell phone rang, and she watched his smooth movements as he answered the call. His gaze never left hers as he spoke a handful of words to whoever was on the other end of the line.

"I'll take care of it. Thank you."

Well, at least he was still cordial. Underneath the Alpha dog was a gentleman. A terrier perhaps. No. A wolf. *Make no mistake, Amanda. He's part wolf. Part animal. A hunter.*

She stepped back again, fear and curiosity warring with the little voice that told her not to give up. Not to give in. Stand tall. But another voice told her that she didn't really know him. She didn't know anything at all. She didn't know what he was, what he was called, did he shift at full moon, at will? What? It was that same little voice that had so long ago urged her to run.

Perhaps it made her a coward, but when it came to her heart she was a coward. Sadly, she could remember the exact day, the exact moment she'd become a coward.

"Thanks for the gumbo." She straightened her spine. "You'll understand if I have your robe sent to you."

With that, she turned and fled the kitchen. She ran across the pine floors toward the front door. She'd crawl through the mud if it meant finding her keys. Clutching the robe around her, she reached for the doorknob.

Strong arms wrapped around her waist and hoisted her into the air.

"Put me down!"

"Not gonna happen, *chèrie*."

"Put me down this instant, Sebastian." Her voice was full of heat and censure.

He slung her over his shoulder enjoying the feel of her small squirming body. He knew he shouldn't get so excited by her helpless struggles, but he couldn't help himself. She beat her small fists against his back as if that would make a difference.

He laughed and nipped at the flesh of her hip. "Not on your life, sweetheart. We've gotta get on the road."

"The road?"

"*Oui*. Hurricane's a comin'. Gotta get the cabin ready. Burke and Laurent are still tied up so that leaves me. Don't want any broken windows." He knew he could've had Jules or André make the drive to batten down the hatches. But the cabin was deeper in the bayou, far enough away for secrets to remain hidden. And he'd already planned on taking care of it himself. Jules comments had given him a lot to think about and he needed some time alone to mull everything over.

But now that Manda was with him…they could get to the bottom of everything.

He had plans for that gorgeous body of hers.

He couldn't wait to feel her feminine curves against him, under him. Her tight sheath around his cock as he slid in and out of her, bringing them both to the brink of ecstasy. The bayou was perfect for what he had in mind and no one could hear her scream his name.

"There's no reason for me to go with you," she insisted, sounding a little more panicked now and a lot more breathless.

"Sure, there is, *chérie*." Sebastian opened the front door and stepped out into the hot damp air.

"I don't think so." She kicked, her knee nailing him in the gut.

"Hold still, woman! I don' wanna hurt you."

That got her attention. She froze atop his shoulder.

He cursed beneath his breath and started down the stairs toward the garage. The rain showered down on them, soaking the thin fabric of his T-shirt, but he hardly noticed.

"You know I would never hurt you, Manda. Do not even think it."

She was silent for several long moments as if she was mulling over his words. Good.

"Just let me go, Sebastian. I have a job, a life in New York!" she pleaded.

"And some boyfriend up there as well, no doubt."

"I don't have a boyfriend."

"Really? No boyfriend." He entered the

garage and pulled his key chain from his pocket. His investigator hadn't reported any man in Amanda's life for several years but hearing the confirmation from her lips was all the sweeter. Did she still pine for him the way he did for her?

"Really. Now. Put. Me. Down!"

"Can't. You've seen too much." That much was true. "And besides, traffic has been grounded at the airport thanks to the storm."

4

The next thing Amanda knew, she was in the back of a Mercedes, the same color as his midnight black hair, with her hands and feet tied. She'd caught a glimpse of the license plate before he'd deposited her in the backseat.

Appropriately, it read ALPHA. She sneered with disgust, partly at him, partly at herself, but mostly at the whole situation.

"I can't believe you tied me up. You big jerk," she yelled as he circled the car. His hands had moved like lightening, imprisoning her wrists with black straps that felt like silk. She tried not to think of why he had them in his car and who he'd used them on before.

He laughed as he landed in the driver's seat and glanced back at her in the rear-view mirror. "So, I'm a jerk and a rat." He sounded amused.

She wanted to wipe the amusement off his

face. For the hundredth time, she wondered what the hell had caused her to drive out to his sprawling estate and get out of her car. She'd lied when she'd told him she hadn't known it was his home. Though she'd been gone almost a decade, she had her sources. And in that decade, he'd made an incredible home for himself and his family. It was huge and impressively restored.

"You cannot keep running away from me, *mon amour*. I won't allow it."

A pang of regret needled her as they pulled away from the beautiful home and lush landscaping.

As a young woman, she'd dreamed of marrying Sebastian, becoming his wife, his lover. Building a home with him…having his babies.

But what had possessed her to hop the fence instead of ringing from the call box? An invisible force had pulled her to him, but she'd needed to know if there was a woman in his life. A steady woman, not the starlets he'd been photographed with over the years.

If he was attached… she couldn't, wouldn't, think about it. The thought hurt too much.

She knew her curiosity had gotten the better of her. That was never going to happen again.

Part of her wanted to give him what for. Which wasn't new; their verbal sparring was one of her favorite memories of their time together. But that had been all spit and fire, not emotion.

At least not on his end. She'd always felt like he was humoring her, perhaps even pitying her because her own parents didn't seem to care whether she was alive or dead in a ditch.

Like so many days, the day before her History final during her junior year was etched into her memory. It'd been hot and so humid her shirt was a limp rag. Mom hadn't been able to pay the bills on time, again, and so the tiny window unit sat quiet. Amanda had abandoned the house in search of cool shade and found it beneath the tree in Sebastian's front yard.

Swamp creatures were just starting to come out after the heat of the day. The Beast, the name she'd secretly given the big black truck Sebastian drove, rolled up and three pairs of shoes hit the ground. Jules was the first to stroll her way.

"Manda, my love, why are ya in da heat?" He glanced up at the sun overhead, but the sunglasses hid his eyes. Didn't matter; she knew how inky dark they were, how easy it was to get lost in them. When he glanced back down at her, there was a hint of concern pinching his brows.

She hated telling them the truth, that her mom had forgotten to pay the bill or that she didn't have enough money to pay it on time. There was always an excuse, an apology, a promise to do better. And then there were the whispers about the Deveraux men, her neighbors.

And she didn't mean the whispers about their animal magnetism or why five bachelors bunked down together. She didn't know what to believe about those stories, so she ignored them. But there were murmurings of how wealthy these men were.

If those rumors were true…she couldn't tell them she didn't have power. She didn't want Sebastian to explode. He seemed to always be looking out for her and she was starting to resent being taken care of like a needy kid sister. Problem was, she was pretty needy.

"You know how I like the fresh air," she quipped. That was so far from the truth, but she spoke with a smile and hoped it fooled them.

Momma insisted on her focusing on school when Amanda had offered to get a job. It took her an hour to walk home from the bus stop. Occasionally she'd get lucky and one of the guys would be coming home early and offer her a lift.

"Fresh air? In da swamp?" Sebastian asked, looking at the black waters across the road. Then she felt the heat of his gaze and tipped her head up. It was impossible to ignore that voice or the pull she felt deep inside.

"Air conditioner's off," André mused quietly, and she shot him a frown.

Though none of them had ever offered to pay the power bill, she could tell they wanted to. Even now, she felt all three of them looking at her, studying her as if they wanted to fix the problem. But it was more than that. Their stares weren't just platonic. They were hot, hot enough to make the Louisiana sun jealous.

She'd finally sprouted boobs last fall and though they'd never been improper or lecherous, she knew they'd noticed. At least someone was enjoying them because she sure didn't.

"What're ya studying?" Sebastian asked, squatting down.

Holy smokes. When he got this close her brain practically short circuited. Legs, hands, forearms, gorgeous hair…she wanted to run her fingers through it. Yes. Kiss those sinful lips and sink her fingers into that hair.

"History," she said, aware how annoyed she sounded.

"What's wrong with dat?" he asked, pushing his sunglasses on top of his head and glancing down at the book in her lap.

"I hate History and my teacher is a dinosaur."

Jules chuckled and settled next to her, leaning against the trunk of the tree.

"But history is important," Sebastian said. "If you do not know the mistakes of the past how can you prevent them?"

She loved it when he sounded all proper and French. He did have a point, but she couldn't resist sparring with him.

"Your theory assumes that men learn from their mistakes. I haven't found that to be true."

Perhaps he had learned from his mistakes. Rather than treating her like a kid sister, he was certainly taking notice of her now. She slouched against the door and stared at the back of his head. As much as she wanted to scream and kick and demand that he untie her, the other part desperately wanted to curl up in his arms and beg him to make love to her.

She was crazy for even thinking it. She'd seen

him with her own eyes... in wolf form. With fur, four paws and a snout. A slow tremor shook her body and she told herself not to be afraid. He'd never hurt her before, why would he start now. But even though she'd believed for years, seeing it, seeing the truth... she couldn't stop trembling.

"You should thank me, *chérie*."

"Why is that?"

"Because I just saved you from having three men at once."

A gasp caught in her throat, but to her surprise and humiliation, she found herself growing damp at the thought. How perverted was that? What was wrong with her?

Sure, she'd been attracted to all three Deveraux brothers when she'd been young. Not to mention his two cousins. What girl wouldn't be? They were what daydreams were made of.

But she was an adult now. She couldn't be thinking about them like that. And certainly not together.

But the thought lingered.

"Forget it Amanda. It's not going to happen," Sebastian said darkly. A crack of thunder drove his point home.

"You're crazy," she chided even as she pressed her thighs together and tried to think of anything but being in bed with the three of them.

"I'm not the one thinking naughty thoughts about screwing three men at once." A jet-black eyebrow rose in a way she found both arrogant and infuriating.

Obviously, he could read her thoughts. The thought should have terrified her more than it did. But at the moment, she was too busy fuming silently, sprawled across the backseat with the bathrobe gaping open. No doubt, passing truckers would get an eyeful. That just pissed her off more. The Sebastian she'd known and loved would've never put her on display like this.

But he was only to the end of his driveway and she could see the fender of her little rental car parked just outside the gate. After he eased the car between the gaping wrought iron he threw it into park and turned back to her.

"Your purse is in the car?" he asked, and she noticed the key ring dangling from his long sensual fingers.

"Sebastian—"

"Don't play with me, Amanda. You will lose."

She licked her lips and decided it was best to choose her battles carefully. The dangerous and determined glint in his eyes told her to tread carefully.

"Yes, my purse is in the passenger's seat."

He was back in a flash, depositing her purse and her small suitcase in the seat next to him. The reality of what he meant to do sank in. He really was whisking her away. But where?

"Tell me something, *chérie*. Why don't you

want to go with me? We have much to discuss, agreed?"

She sucked in a deep breath, her emotions all over the place. "You want to talk?"

"Not really. But we should, yes?"

"What's there to talk about?" He'd said the only important thing years ago.

"Everything," he said simply and stepped on the gas. The single word sounded so ominous, almost as if she'd done something wrong. But she'd done nothing wrong, except fall for a man who…well, he wasn't even really a man, now was he?

"This is kidnapping," she said finally, breaking the silent treatment.

"I've been accused of worse."

"I don't doubt it," she replied hotly. The stormy clouds overhead had nothing on the intensity of the man in the front seat. He glanced at her in the mirror, as if questioning her sanity. She rolled her eyes and rested her check against the soft leather of the back seat. It smelled of leather and wet dog. *Figured.*

After what seemed like hours, she struggled into a sitting position. At least, she was halfway sitting. Sebastian had been very careful as he'd tied her, even though she hadn't made it easy on him.

Why hadn't she simply promised to stay put? It wasn't as if she was stupid enough to dive out of a moving car but in that moment when he'd first deposited her on the seat and asked her if she promised not to run she'd shaken her head.

Perhaps it was the closeness or maybe it was pheromones, all she knew was being so close to him, feeling his touch, breathing in the raw, masculine scent of him made her a little crazy.

Nothing had changed in that regard. If anything, his power over her body seemed more acute.

She tugged her wrists apart and tried to undo the knot. The straps dug into her skin, and she lost feeling to her fingers. She craved the freedom to move. Craved circulation.

Why was he taking her with him? So, what if the flights were grounded. Certainly, she was safe in a hotel. She didn't want to be in some shack when Hurricane Camilla roared ashore. The man was crazy. Certifiable. Irresistible.

She stared at his strong jaw and had the strongest urge to run her fingertips over the shadow of stubble there.

"You can let me go, you know."

"I cannot."

"Why not?"

"Because you'll run."

"We're back to that?" She sighed and glanced out the window. Dark clouds hung low in the sky and rain pelted them. The windshield wipers were working overtime as they sped south.

"I'm not going to jump out of the car when you slow down to make a turn, if that's what you're worried about." She met his gaze in the rearview mirror.

"I'm just basing my decision on history."

"I didn't have any other choice. You wouldn't understand."

"Try me, *chérie*."

Did he have to use that sweet accent of his? Or call her *darling*? Surely, he knew his endearments, as natural as they were, made her heart flutter.

It shouldn't flutter at all. She should be mad as heck. A few days ago, she'd had the hottest job in New York city, a closet full of great shoes that she could barely afford, and a life without Sebastian. Without his brooding good looks and heart-tripping endearments she'd had her heart firmly in her chest. There'd been no chance of him ripping it from her and stomping on it.

There was no chance of her breaking down and begging for any scrap of affection he could offer her.

Now she was tied in the backseat of his car. With no shoes and only a scrap of her dignity. So why wasn't she spitting mad?

Something was definitely wrong. Maybe she'd hit her head when she'd fallen off his porch. Maybe he'd enchanted her. Did werewolves have magical powers like that? She'd heard rumors...

"What are you thinking about in that beautiful head of yours?"

"Flattery will get you nowhere."

She had to stay strong. Use what little bit of strength and anger she had left. Being this close to him put her in serious danger of falling for his temptation. Falling under his spell. It was lust. She had to remember that. That's all he was offering…*since he wasn't going to marry her.*

"That's not true. Your pulse leapt the tiniest little bit when I called you beautiful. You can't deny it, Manda. Any more than you can deny your desire for me."

She huffed. Of course, she desired him. She'd have to be blind not to. It ticked her off that he read her so easily. She was too obvious in her attraction, probably always had been. As a young woman it'd been hard not to find the handsome men fascinating. And while normally she would be pleased to find a man so in tune with her, that perception, that cunning instinct made him all the more dangerous.

"You're full of it," she scoffed.

"You deny it?"

Before she could answer, he pulled the car to a stop on the shoulder. The sudden movement tossed her forward. The second the car was in park, he was out of his seat and opening the back door. Her heart thundered in her chest. He had a dangerous look in his eyes. Water droplets pelted his shirt, clung to his hair.

Somehow, he folded himself into the backseat and then pulled her into his lap.

"What're you doing?" A shiver raced up her spine. He was too close. Much too close. He would surely read all the secrets in her eyes. Years of hopeless, complete heart-body-and-soul love that wouldn't go away in this lifetime or the next. She owed him so much, wanted him too much.

She looked away.

"Look at me, *chérie*."

She shook her head.

Patiently, he cupped her cheek in his hand. Dear God, she wanted to rub against it, wanted to feel his hands in her hair, his fingers against her lips, her skin, her breasts. This was madness. She'd come down here for a funeral, for goodness sakes. This…this seduction wasn't part of the plan.

Reluctantly she met his eyes. Damn if he wasn't the most potent thing on two legs.

"That's better." He stared at her as if searching for something. "Now tell me you don't desire me."

Looking at him made her stomach do little cartwheels. She was so tired of denying the truth, denying her desire for him, trying to give equal attention to all five Deveraux men. She was tired of protecting herself all the time, of trying too damn hard not to be her mother. Mostly she was tired of feeling alone in a city of millions. Even though they weren't related by blood, she'd always thought of the Deverauxs as her family. Her men.

She shook her head again, unable to say the words aloud, but couldn't help leaning into him. His hand stroked her side through the thick material of his robe and she yearned to remove the barrier, to be naked in his arms, to feel his skin against hers.

"That's right. You can't say it. It's not true. You've always wanted me, *mon amour*. Just as I've always wanted you."

Her eyes swerved up. He'd always wanted her? What about what he'd said to Jules?

She started to speak but the words came out in a jumbled heap. The chill bumps came back full force and she shivered beneath the thick robe.

"Shh..." His gaze flicked to her lips and she licked them quickly, hoping, praying he'd kiss her. Their breath mingled. God, how she'd dreamed of this. Of being this close.

"Desire was never our problem, was it?" he whispered.

Desire could easily be swayed by the brain, by knowledge of what was right and wrong or morals. Love. Love was their problem. He had hers. All of hers. Even now, one hour in his company again and she feared she'd been lying to herself since the day she'd run away.

"We need to get back on the road. Don't wanna get stuck out here with the storm a comin'."

He kissed her forehead and lifted her from his lap. That was it? *That was all?*

He came back here and told her how much he wanted her? And didn't even steal a kiss?

"Men," she mumbled, needy and unfulfilled.

She wanted to scream. She wanted to tell him to get back here and put her out of a dozen years of lust-filled misery.

ONCE BEHIND THE WHEEL, Sebastian pressed his foot down hard on the pedal, hoping the tires wouldn't slip on the water.

His resolve was in jeopardy. He'd simply meant to prove to her that she couldn't lie to him, show her that he knew her as well as she knew herself. He could see in her eyes how much she wanted him.

Maybe it hadn't been such a good idea to bring her down here to the middle of nowhere. If he'd stayed at his estate, he could already be inside her sweet body.

Damn. Damn. Double damn.

His cock was rock hard. Thankfully, they'd be at the cabin soon. He had to get control of himself.

Manda grumbled to herself. He couldn't quite

make out what she said, but a look in the mirror told him she was fuming.

"What's got yer feathers ruffled, *chérie*?"

"You! You, Sebastian. Always playing God. You've kidnapped me. Tied my hands and feet. As if I'm going somewhere."

"You're still denying that you ran away from me nine years ago?"

"I ran away from everything," she cried. Surprised at her outburst, he looked back at her again. Even in the murky light, he could see pink staining her cheeks.

"From you. From here. These people. The memories."

"Why, Manda?"

"I didn't want to end up like my mom," she shouted, tears tumbling down her cheeks.

What?

He saw his turn coming up and gently pressed the break. Just another minute. Then they were getting to the bottom of this.

Spotting the cabin on the left, he flipped the blinker and pulled into the driveway.

"You call this a cabin?" Manda asked, her gaze fixed on the wide wooden structure.

"A fishing cabin, *oui*. My brothers, cousins and I each have a key." He steered his Mercedes around the side of the house and up the steep drive. A button on the dash opened the garage door. When they were safely inside, he turned the car off and then glanced over his shoulder at her.

She stared at him wide eyed, then shook her head.

"Now tell me, *cher*, how did your mother end up?"

"Please. As if you don't know. She was the laughing stock of Louisiana."

He raised an eyebrow at that. Her mother had always been warm and friendly. Even when he and his brothers kept snooping around her daughter. His own mother had never been warm or friendly toward him. But then he'd always wondered if Ms. St. James had known the truth about her neighbors. Like most folks out this way, she had a healthy superstitious bone.

"How so?"

She let out a frustrated sigh, as if explaining was either painful or beneath her. "Are you going to untie me?"

He draped his arm over the back of the passenger's seat and regarded her slowly. She writhed beneath his gaze just as he wanted her to. He wanted her on edge, white hot with lust. Because he intended to have her very, very soon. For a very, very, very long time.

"Not until you tell me what I want to know."

Being tied up kept an adorable, and pouty, frown on her lips which kept his libido in check. Well, slightly in check because heaven help him, he hadn't known a peaceful night since that first hot summer day when he'd laid eyes on her for the first time.

"You're insufferable."

"Why didn't you want to be like your mom? She was nice. Caring."

"She loved a man who never loved her back."

He looked in her eyes and could see her pain.

"What do you mean, *cher*?" He didn't understand. His parents had never been in love but that didn't stop him from wanting it. Wanting her.

"My dad never loved my mother. He had relationships behind her back constantly and they broke up. We moved out, but she never got over him. He'd come visit, act as if they were going to work things out and—" her voice broke off. "You saw how he was."

True. Her father, the skunk, had driven out to the little shanty where his daughter lived more often than not without electricity in a shiny BMW. He was obviously doing well for himself. As far as Sebastian knew, he'd never laid a finger on Amanda. Her mother wasn't so lucky. He got the impression that her clinginess would set the man off. Despite the distance, through the walls, Sebastian's keen ears had heard the feminine cries. After reining in his beast he'd stepped outside and stared the bastard down. The SOB had never come back.

"Do you think a person can die from a broken heart?"

So that's why she'd only come back when her father died. As far as he knew, they hadn't seen each other in the nine years she'd been gone. And now that her dad was dead, well, she didn't seem entirely upset about it. If anything, attending his funeral would prove that the bastard was dead.

Damn, he wished he'd known that she'd been comparing herself to her mother all these years. He would have been there for her.

"I don't know, *cher*."

"She loved him more than anything and he didn't even show up for her funeral."

Puzzle pieces started to fall into place. So that's why she'd run. She'd thought her feelings, her desires, were one sided.

He didn't see how. He'd always craved her. *Women never made sense to him. Especially human women. They expected men to read their minds. Afraid to say what they wanted, take what they wanted.*

She brushed the hair from her eyes and he caught sight of her bound wrists.

"Hold that thought." He got out of the car and went to turn on the overhead light. While the garage door rumbled closed, he opened her door.

"Promise not to run?" he asked.

"Never," she said but her words lacked conviction. She wiggled toward the edge of the seat.

The bathrobe gaped, showing off her creamy

skin. Just a little farther and he'd be able to see her breasts. *Veuillez Dieu.* She caught him looking at her and frowned up at him. She was terribly cute with her pouty lips and crinkled forehead. Her long hair was disheveled around her face, almost dry now despite the humidity.

"Let me help you," he whispered and gathered her in his arms. She didn't make a sound, merely held herself rigid.

As he carried her up the stairs into the house, brilliant blue lightning lit the sky. Silently he counted the seconds until he heard the first crack of thunder.

"Storm's movin' fast. Forgive me *cher*. We'll finish our talk as soon as I have things stowed away," he murmured against her cheek, reluctant to let her go. He felt and heard her sharp intake of breath. *So, she wasn't as unmoved as she wanted him to think.*

That made it even harder to put her down, to step away from her, when all he wanted to do was strip her down and touch her everywhere. Kiss and lick until he'd explored every inch of her body.

A quick gust of wind buffeted the south side of the cabin and a patio chair tumbled by the French doors. He left her standing in front of the leather sofa in the living room and went to find the candles and flashlights. He deposited those on the coffee table in front of her and then went to bring the patio furniture in off the deck.

Her gaze followed him the whole time. He could feel the tension growing between them along with her impatience. But he could smell her desire. He knew that once he dipped into her he wouldn't be able to stay afloat.

"You can have a seat, you know," he told her as he passed by with the last of the chairs.

"I have to pee," she said between gritted teeth.

"Well, then... We do have a bathroom here. We're not totally primitive." He let the last word hang in the air.

Her eyebrows shot skyward.

"It's through that door over there." He pointed.

"And how am I going to get there? Hop like a rabbit?"

Her sassy response made him smile. Damn, he'd missed her. André was right. He was a fool. Sometimes he was stuck in his own world and needed a good smack upside the head.

"You do remind me of a bunny..." he mused, stalking closer. She was soft, gentle and right now she looked wide eyed like a rabbit who'd just spotted a wolf. No doubt she was ready to dart at a moment's notice.

"But I don't mind carrying you." He couldn't stop his gaze from roaming over the creamy flesh, starkly pale against the midnight black of his robe.

She had no idea just how he wanted to gobble her up, nibble every delicate spot from her ears to her toes.

"If you'd just untie me—"

"*Non.* You will run. Then I'll chase. And I'll bring you back. You'll just wear yourself out, *petite.*"

"Why are you doing this? Why are you trying to keep me here?"

"I should think it obvious," he whispered in her ear. He rubbed his cheek against hers and then lifted her into his arms. He strode across the room to the knotty pine door and nudged it open with his foot. He let her down gently and smiled at her frown.

When he started to leave, she called after him frantically.

"*Oui, mon amour?*"

"Untie me. Now!"

"Sorry. No can do. Here. I'll help though, yes?" He cocked an eyebrow and gathered the robe in his hands. How he loved to tease her. How he wanted to please her, pleasure her in every way he could think of. But she had to learn how to trust him first.

Manda's eyebrows shot up and she grabbed onto his arm with her hands, bound at the wrists.

"Don't look," she ordered.

"Why not, *chérie?* You have nothing I have not seen."

"You've never seen me naked," she whispered fiercely.

He chuckled. That was a problem he intended to remedy very shortly. "I'll turn my head," he told her sweetly.

The tiny bit of gentleman left in him said to simply untie her. But the darker side of him took perverse pleasure in her slow submission.

With her hands and feet bound, she flopped down on the toilet.

"I can't believe this," she grumbled.

"You must learn that I'll take care of you *chérie*."

"Why?"

"A husband always takes care of his wife."

5

Sebastian left her sitting there wide-eyed. He figured she'd call him to help her up, but she didn't say a word for endless minutes. She was either confused as hell or hoppin' mad. He wasn't sure which. As he lowered the storm shutters, he figured he'd find out soon.

Finally, she called his name followed by "untie me you brute. I have to wipe." He could see her grinding her jaws together and her eyes glistening. For a brief second, he feared he'd pushed her too far. He conceded and untied her wrists then stepped from the room and crossed his arms over his chest. Patience wasn't his strong suit.

"What did you mean by 'a husband always takes care of his wife?'" she called a minute later as the toilet flushed.

"Just what I said."

"We aren't married."

At her heated retort, he opened the door and pulled her against him. "But we will be."

"Says who?"

"Says me. I can have Judge Rothburn here in a few minutes."

"A few minutes!" She sounded panicked. "He can't see me like this. Sebastian, untie me this minute!" Her old accent was starting to come out. As if suddenly realizing that her hands were free she bent and started frantically working the knots.

"Manda—"

She was free, glancing at the front door.

"Don't even think about it, *chérie*."

"Too late," she whispered back, mocking him.

"Don't forget, *petite*, that I have excellent night vision. If you run, I will hunt you down."

"You didn't before," Amanda tossed back.

Before he could reach for her she strode up the stairs toward the bedrooms. But he saw the sheen of tears in her eyes. He started after her but halfway up she stopped and turned back to him.

"I'm not running away Sebastian. I just—I need a minute. Would you mind bringing in my suitcase?"

He stared at her for a long moment, looking for signs of deception and found none. She simply looked overwhelmed with emotion.

"Of course, *chérie*."

. . .

Amanda continued up the stairs hoping to find a bedroom where she could have a few minutes to herself. To cool down because inside she was on fire. Sebastian's words had brought all too familiar pictures to her mind. Familiar and seductive. The image of herself fleeing into the darkness with him hot on her heels was a dream she'd had hundreds of times.

It always ended the same way...

Eventually he would catch her, his hands biting into her flesh as he hauled her against him. She was too tired to put up a fight. In fact, she almost sagged with relief. His body was big and strong and warm. The warmth she craved.

He turned her toward him roughly, tearing off her clothes with desperate hands. His eyes glowed a beautiful silver. He made no effort to hide his erection, made no move to release it.

Instead, he caressed her, running his hands over every inch that he could reach. Her skin was taut with goose bumps and his touch slowly warmed her, made her wet with desire.

Without a word, he stepped back, and his clothes disappeared like magic. In the darkness, she had a hard time taking in the view but knew he was solid and strong. His cock was long and thick, jutting out towards her.

Momentarily panicked, she backed away, but he was on her in an instant. They fell through the air, rolling on the damp ground. She found herself on her stomach, her breasts pressed painfully into the earth with Sebastian's hot breath on the back of her neck.

"Tell me you want me," he whispered into the darkness.

A gargled sound escaped her lips.

He pushed his weight off her and she instantly missed the warm shield his body had provided.

"Tell me you want me," he said again.

Oh, God help her. She'd always wanted him. For years, she'd wanted him to claim her, to take her body. To bring her pleasure.

"Say it," he ordered, pulling her up on her hands and knees. She wobbled, feeling completely exposed. His hands smoothed over her backside, his palms cupping every curve. "I know you want me, petite. You're on fire for me. I bet you're dripping for me."

His thumbs skimmed her pussy lips. She could feel the wetness, knew that he could feel it too, and that she couldn't deny it. Her nipples hardened in the cool air and she shivered again.

"You can't deny it, little one. Your body gives you away. You want me just as badly as I want you."

He probed her pussy with a single thick finger. It wasn't nearly enough. She craved more.

She pushed back against his hand shamelessly, moaning low in her throat. He laughed then showered kisses along her spine. A warm hand closed over her left breast, cupping its weight. Slowly, he massaged the pointed peak and began driving his finger into her. Then two fingers.

Then three. He stretched her, but it still wasn't enough. Her skin was aflame for him and she wanted to come more than she wanted her next breath.

His hand left her breast and flicked over her clit. The tiny bolt of electricity shot through her body causing her to mewl, but she spread her legs wider, trying to rub against his fingers. She didn't care if anyone came upon them, if anyone saw how exposed she was. It didn't matter that she was naked in the middle of the forest, or that there were probably bugs and animals lurking all around her. She could only think of his strong hands and that thick cock.

"Say it, petite." His voice was harsh and filled with frustration. She wanted to tease him. To make him admit his feelings for her. To make him pleasure her until she came. But when he pulled his fingers from her wetness she forgot all about her plans. She could only cry out at the emptiness.

"I won't touch you again until you—"

"Fuck me, Sebastian!"

He immediately slid the broad tip of his cock inside her, answering her desperate cry. He worked himself inside inch by slow inch. He was so thick. So long. Was he going to fit?

A few seconds later, he pulled out and thrust all the way in, delighting every nerve along the way. A happy gasp left her throat. His hands clasped her hips tightly, holding her steady as he increased the tempo.

"You're so wet. So tight." Above her, he grunted and groaned as he pumped in and out. His balls slapped

against her clit in a rhythm that tortured and teased her. He pushed her closer and closer to the brink. She tightened her muscles around him, reveling in the deep groan that erupted from his lips.

He wrapped himself around her, and even as his cock filled her and her pleasure teased her with its nearness, she marveled in how big he was. How strong. And how feminine she felt next to him, under him.

He pulled all the way out and she felt emptier than ever before. A searching finger teased her clit and drew lazy circles keeping her at her peak.

"Please," she moaned and leaned down slightly hoping he would let her come.

He drove into her with a force that startled a cry from her lips and almost toppled her. Furiously he pounded her pussy and rubbed her clit.

Her orgasm was explosive. Not the usual wave that washed over her. But a bomb of pleasure exploding inside her and radiating outward. His cries joined hers and she felt him swell inside her tender sheath. His movements halted but she could feel him coming, could feel every muscle tightening like a violin string.

She was always amazed at his stamina. At least his stamina in her dreams. He would fuck her until she couldn't stand up. So, they'd simply lay down. She'd curl around him and he would stroke her skin with gentle hands, telling her that it was only the beginning. Murmuring words of love...

The power picked that moment to go out, startling Amanda from her daydream. A startled squeak escaped her lips and she rushed into the nearest room where the eerie gray/green evening light filtered through a window.

"Manda," Sebastian called. "Are you all right, *chérie*?"

So, he had super sensitive hearing. Figured.

"Here *chérie*, I already had the candles out," Sebastian murmured, entering the room with a single pillar candle aflame.

She watched, mute, as he lowered the shutters and moved to the next room to do the same. Darkness fell, brightened by the single dancing flame that gave the bedroom a romantic glow. Heaven help her.

"Now let us finish the conversation we started—"

His deep voice startled her from her wayward thoughts.

"Why did you send me flowers? Why did you write that note?" she asked determined to say what needed saying. No more running away. No more taking the coward's way out. If he wasn't head over heels for her then she would find some way to move on. Maybe New York wasn't far enough away. There was always London. Or Siberia.

. . .

Swiftly, he pulled her to him and stared down into her upturned face. "I never sent you flowers."

"Yes, you did. You signed them 'love, Sebastian.' But you obviously didn't mean it. You just want to get your way, like always. Like the time you whisked me away to the Oak Alley Plantation so that your brothers couldn't. You didn't want me alone with them. Admit that you want me, so your brothers can't have me."

"I always get my way, Manda." He pressed her hips against hers and cupped her cheek, tipping her chin up until she met his gaze. "That's why I'm Alpha. And I do love you, I think I always have. But I didn't send you flowers. And I don't want you just so my brothers can't have you."

Her jaw dropped, and tears dripped down her cheeks. Outside, a clap of thunder sounded. It shook the walls and hurt his ears.

Her laugh was harsh and hollow. She pulled away from him, but he couldn't fathom why. She reached out for the dresser to steady herself.

"Why now? Why do you tell me this now?" Her voice rose, and she broke off in string of crazy, jumbled French.

"What's wrong, *mon amour*? Why are you crying?"

He wondered if he'd ever understand women. *Tell them what they want to hear and they cry. Don't tell them and they cry anyway.* All he knew was that his cock was hard as a damn rock, his heart was pounding like the rain, and there was a hurricane coming ashore. He really needed to finish battening down the hatches, but Amanda was more important than busted windows.

"I'm crying for all the years we wasted."

"That's it?" He mourned that too, but nine years out of his lifetime was worth the wait if she'd be in his arms every day for the rest of it.

The thought of waking up next to her each day made his heart ache with happiness. He could almost see the days laid out like photographs in front of him. There didn't seem to be enough. But he'd always known that if he chose a human for a mate his life would be tied to hers. When she died, he would as well.

The happiness in his heart turned to anguish. A brutal, scalding ache. He studied her, remembering the first time she'd looked at him like he was her hero. He'd known right then that he'd fight to the death for her. And if finally having her meant shortening his life… he took a deep steadying breath, hardly able to believe that the day was here, and he was making this decision. It was a decision all alphas had to make sometime; a sacrifice his brothers and the pack understood.

"That's it? That's it!" she demanded, her voice hoarse from crying. "Tell me right now, Sebastian or I'm running out of here and you'll never see me again. Why do you want to marry me? Why so suddenly?

"All the time I was growing up you had mood swings that could rival any woman with PMS. You'd look at me like I was your entire world. And the next minute you'd treat me like a kid sister. Or worse. You wouldn't say anything at all. You'd fight with your brothers—

She took a quick breath and continued her tirade, "I heard what you said to Jules that day. About how you could 'never marry me.' That was the last straw for me. I was so damn confused all the time that I had to leave. I had to get away. I never knew where you stood. All I knew was that I was crazy in love with you, and for some reason or other, you didn't feel the same way. Or maybe you had demons to exorcise. I don't know.

"So, I repeat. Why now? Why in the middle of a hurricane? After all these years... Why didn't you come after me? Why didn't you call? Track me down? Hunt me down if you're so darn good at it?"

When she paused to take a breath, he held up his hand. Stunned only began to define what he was feeling. It was like when he'd become Alpha of the pack. All the love and responsibility stared him straight in the face.

He'd never known lil' Amanda St. James had such a set of lungs. Her eyes were so earnest, so brilliant despite the darkness that he was momentarily mesmerized.

"Are you gonna answer the girl or not?" Burke's voice cut through the air.

"Cause if you don', I'm gonna come up there and steal her away, cousin," Laurent added.

Amanda's gaze swerved to the stairs. "Wha—"

Sebastian snarled, low and long, annoyed that he'd been so wrapped up in their conversation that he hadn't heard his cousins arrive. Amanda backed away from the menacing sound.

"You're not going to touch her," Sebastian told the men standing on the stairs. Burke's lips twitched, and Laurent shot him a knowing smile.

Laurent laughed. "Yer right."

"We were going to prepare for the storm, but it looks like you've taken care of things, cousin," Burke added, a brow raised.

Sebastian sighed. He wondered which one of them had won the bet as to when Sebastian would finally go after Amanda and pop the question. Right now, he didn't really mind that they'd wagered on his love life. The only thing that really mattered was making Amanda his wife as soon as possible. He couldn't wait any longer to stake his claim in all possible ways.

"One of you call Judge Rothburn. I want to marry this woman before that hurricane gets here."

"Se—" Manda started.

He held a finger against her lips, imploring her with his eyes. "We have a lot of time to make up for, starting now."

Then he got down on his knees and reached for her.

"Chalk it up to foolish pride, *chérie*. We wolv—" he caught his slip of the tongue just in time, "men aren't the smartest in the food chain when it comes to things like this.

"But I've always wanted you. You always make me laugh. You keep me grounded. You make me want to do better at everything. When you smile, I feel like I can do anything in the world. You make me more human."

He took a deep breath. "When I said those words to Jules I was trying to convince myself, remind myself of your age and innocence. I'm not known for my patience. I am however known for my possessiveness."

He kneaded her hips with his hands, willing her to understand how he'd felt that day nine years ago. It was hard to put his struggle into words.

"You were so young, and I had no business—"

"Don't give me that, Sebastian. You weren't just some creep in the neighborhood getting his jollies by watching the girl next door."

"Oh, Manda…" That's exactly what he'd been. "Did you know what the day we met, I'd been driving by on detour? That I saw you sitting on your front porch and I was so drawn to you that we moved in that same day? All I knew, petite, was that you were going to be special. I had to be near you."

"Don't. Don't degrade what we had. You were my family, my friend. The whole lot of you. Y'all were there for me when no one else was. That awful rainstorm March of my Junior year? Who picked me up so I didn't have to walk home in it?"

"I did."

"And who looked after me after my mom died?"

"We did."

"Are you seeing the pattern?"

He nodded.

"You could have married me that day. You could have had me any way you wanted. I was completely devoted to you Sebastian. How could you not know that?"

"I did."

Her eyebrows arched. "Then—"

"Because, I wanted to make sure you were in it for the long haul. I had to make sure it wasn't some passing fancy—"

"Passing fancy," she screeched.

"Or that you'd grow up and away from us. You wanted a career. You wanted out of the bayou—"

"Don't you dare pin that on me." She stalked toward the window.

"The only reason I left was because I overhead you tell your brother that you wouldn't marry me and that he wasn't going to either."

Her eyes seemed to glow. Not with anger or confusion, or even lust. But something else. Something that took his breath away.

"It was like looking in the mirror and seeing my mother's life flashing before my eyes. I'd thought you were different—"

"I am!"

"I knew you cared about me. I knew we had something special. Something that defied age, time or reason. I didn't need years of life experience to tell me that we had a connection, a bond so unique that it was a once in a thousand lifetimes kind of gift."

Sebastian's heart stuttered at her words, at her beautiful defiance. She was the most gorgeous creature he'd ever known, could ever hope to know. He ached because of the pain he'd caused her. The anguish in her voice stabbed him like a million little daggers.

"But you broke my heart that day, Bastian. You cracked my soul and I wasn't going to wait around for you to do it over and over again."

He pulled her into his arms, needing to feel her against him.

"I wasn't running from you Sebastian. Not really."

He held her tighter, everything making sense now. "Forgive me, *mon amour*. I—"

"I'll forgive you, Mr. Deveraux," she said, a teasing light in her eyes. "But you still have some explaining to do." She smiled up at him. "And an important question to ask."

The air stalled in his lungs. He knew what she was asking, what she needed to know. But he couldn't tell her, that would change everything. The truth would terrify her, and he'd rather die than have her disappear from his life again.

Maybe he could keep that part of him in check; she'd never have to see him in his true form.

As much as he liked the idea of protecting her, he hated the idea of lying to her.

"Show me Sebastian." She grazed a finger down his cheek, her beautiful blue eyes locked with his. Too much, she was too much, too good, too good to be true. "You know you can trust me, right?"

"You don't know what you're asking."

"I'm asking for the truth. We can't be together, really together with the trust required to build a life together if you can't share everything you are with me. I've seen too many lives torn apart by deception, Sebastian. Too many marriages ripped apart by lies and omissions. I want to know all of you, everything about you."

"This will change everything."

"I hope so."

"But it will *change* things between us, your feelings for me. Don't you understand? I can't live without you anymore."

"You were doing a fine job of it the last nine years. I saw your photo in the paper."

"That was existing."

"Trust me, Sebastian. I opened my heart to you. It's time you returned the favor. Since there's no full moon, I take it…"

"I'll explain it all later. Don't hate me, Manda."

He stepped back, crouched on the floor and let the change take him. It took more courage than he thought he had but she was right. They needed absolute truth between them. That was hard for a man who'd lived in the shadows for so long.

She sucked in a slow breath and her heartbeat accelerated but he didn't dare look at her. He kept his gaze focused on the floor at her feet and prayed that the gods would finally let him catch a break.

In all his years he'd never shown his true self to any human; he hoped that he hadn't made a colossal mistake. As he shifted, she didn't move, didn't speak. Why didn't she scream? Run? Something. Anything.

A small hand appeared at the end of his snout and her delicious feminine scent filled his lungs. He nuzzled her skin and she slowly turned her hand over. He licked her palm and felt her shiver.

To his utter amazement, he smelled no fear in her.

She cupped his jaw and applied pressure until he looked up at her. He felt the scrutiny in her gaze, knew she was searching for the man inside the wolf. He was here, right here.

The smile that slowly crept across her face was radiant and it stole his breath. "Now, about that question."

He stared at her for endless seconds, until he was sure he was dreaming. She barely blinked and she didn't remove her hand. Rather she scratched beneath his ears.

And then all at once reality sank in. She wasn't rejecting him.

He shifted back, his clothes in tatters at his feet. Not feeling the least bit modest, he knelt on one knee and reached for her hand. He felt clumsy and ready to explode with joy.

"Marry me, Amanda. You're the most incredible woman I've ever met, and I don't want to live without you."

"Was that in the form of a question?" Her eyes were bright with mischief.

"Woman—"

"Of course, I'll marry you, Sebastian. Seems I've waited my whole life to do just that."

———

AFTER THE JUDGE and his cousins had left, he pulled his wife toward him. The somewhat chaste kiss he'd given her moments ago when Rothburn had uttered those sweet words ordering him to kiss his bride...well, that wasn't nearly enough to satisfy him. He'd been waiting over two hundred years for this, for his mate, his wife. Across two continents and an ocean, but he'd finally found her. Finally made her his.

"I want you," he murmured. He gently clasped her face between his hands and gazed into her eyes. "I've wanted you so long, *chérie*. So long. And you disappeared from my life. Never again." He lowered his head and brushed his lips against hers. The first touch was gentle, sweet. The slightest of caresses. Having tested the waters, he caressed her cheeks with his thumbs and deepened the kiss. His tongue slid along the seam of her lips, begging entrance. She took little convincing and soon he was inside, plunging into her. Taking her.

She whimpered when he pulled back. He tipped his forehead against hers and stared into her eyes again.

"You know I'll never let you go now."

Now that she was his wife, she wasn't going anywhere. She felt stronger, happier, completely secure for the first time in her life. It was a feeling she could get used to.

His hands tightened around her waist and she pressed closer, tangling her fingers in his hair.

Dear God, he was her husband now. It was amazing. Was it three days ago, she'd been in New York? It felt like a lifetime. She took a moment to take it all in. He'd said the words she'd always longed to hear. And she knew he spoke the truth.

Sebastian wasn't one to spout his feelings. Perhaps that had been their problem all along. Hormones. Lack of communication. And a possessive streak as wide as the Mississippi.

"Am I dreaming?" she asked, lazily trailing her fingernails along his scalp.

"If you are, I hope you never wake up."

His hand traced the length of her spine leaving a delicious chill in its wake. His eyes burned bright in the soft glow. Outside the storm raged and a haunting wind howled through the trees. Amanda had never been this far south during a hurricane. One thing her mother'd always done right was evacuate to higher ground. Would this place withstand the wind? The water?

"It's sturdy, *mon amour*."

Sometimes, she really did wonder if he could

read her mind. He gave her a reassuring smile that had her stomach doing cartwheels.

It seemed surreal—the candles, the storm, their whirlwind wedding—she could barely believe she was standing in the same room with Sebastian, much less married to him. But she wasn't dreaming. His kiss had been far too good to be a dream. She smiled at him as she pressed her hips against his erection.

He groaned and scooped her up into his arms.

6

They'd barely made it back to the bedroom before Sebastian had slipped the delicate pink wrap-dress from her shoulders. She'd insisted that she couldn't get married in his bathrobe.

The soft material pooled around her waist, giving him easy access to her full breasts. He trailed his hands over her collarbone before cupping the sweet flesh in his hands. As he caressed each curve, he memorized every delicious detail. Every catch of her breath. Every skip of her pulse beneath his fingertips.

Her hands tugged at his shirt. He barely noticed. He knew nothing but the hard, little peaks between his fingers. He squeezed gently, and Manda moaned into the darkness.

"Like that, do you, *cher?*"

"Mmm hmm."

He dipped his head and laved one of the

dusky pink nipples with his tongue. God, she smelled heavenly. Aroused...warm...feminine. His cock twitched behind the seam of his jeans.

"I want to touch you," she whispered into the darkness.

Quickly, he tugged his shirt over his head and went back to loving her breasts. She shimmied and squirmed as he rolled the sensitive nubs between his thumb and finger. When he tugged, she actually screamed. The sound echoed off the walls only to be drowned out by the intense rain outside.

Her nails raked over his back and she tried to rub against him. He held her at bay. If she touched him much more, he'd come in his pants.

"Hurry," she pleaded.

"Hurry, *petite*? Why should I hurry?"

"I want to touch you. I've dreamed—"

He leaned forward and traced her earlobe with his tongue. A shiver racked her body and her skin tightened beneath his hands.

"What have you dreamed?" he whispered.

She hid her face against his neck, her arms wrapped tightly around him.

She felt so good in his arms. So right. Just the right size. With a flick of his wrist, the dress fell away, and she was completely naked. Gloriously, beautifully naked. And wet. He could smell her desire.

"Tell me," he said softly and slid a hand

between her legs. Her hair was short there, her skin soft. He couldn't wait to see her in the daylight when he could drink in every detail.

"I've dreamed of you. That's all."

"What did we do in these dreams?"

Instead of answering, she ran her hands over the hard muscles of his chest. He let his head fall back as he relished her touch. Her small slender hands were cool and soft. He wanted to suck on every finger…see exactly what turned her on. What made her fall apart.

Her hands slid lower, down his abs and straight to the ridge in his jeans. She cupped his cock as if testing the size. He could hear her breath coming in shallow pants now. Cupping her cheeks, he dove into her mouth, his tongue dancing between her lips.

She gasped at the invasion. Slowly her hand squeezed his cock, bringing him closer to the edge.

"Amanda," he rumbled. She didn't heed his warning; instead, continued to tempt and test him.

"What?" she asked innocently, even as she pressed herself against him.

Damn she felt good. Soft, sexy… perfect. Her nipples rubbed against his skin and his cock leapt against her hand.

"You need to keep your hands to yourself." He didn't know how much longer he could last. He liked to pride himself on his endurance. But Manda was special. He'd been waiting for her for a very long time.

He'd dreamed of how their first time would be, off and on for years. Even before it had been decent to do so. But this is not how he'd imagined it. He'd had more control. It wouldn't do to come in his pants like a horny teenager.

"That's not fair. I've wanted to touch you since the first time I saw you without your shirt on years ago." Her admission was quiet, husky, but it had an effect on him nevertheless.

"You still haven't told me what I want to know." He scooped her up and deposited her on the bed. "Don't move," he said.

He practically ran to the living room to get the ropes he'd tied her with earlier. There was no way he was going to give in and fuck her fast and hard. He wanted things nice and slow. But that would never happen if she kept touching him.

He wanted to devour every inch of her.

Kiss the undersides of her breasts.

Lick her pussy dry.

Nibble his way down her thighs all the way to her toes.

"What are you doing?" she called.

"Tyin' ya up, *chérie*."

"Why?" She sounded slightly panicked.

He returned and leaned down to kiss her on the cheek. When she saw the rope in his hands, her eyes squinted, and he could tell she was more angry than panicked.

"You are not tying me up again Sebastian."

"You can't touch me, not yet. I'm too on edge—"

"I want you on edge," she said, her voice almost a purr.

"Dammit, Amanda. You make me crazy. I've never been this hard before, and I don't want to hurt you. You're small and sweet and delicate and I'm tough and—"

"But I want you all hard and tough." She teased his nipples with her fingertips and he stifled a groan. She didn't understand what she was messing with. His baser instincts were barely in check.

"You say that but—" he trailed off, half afraid of something he couldn't even put a name to.

"What?"

"I don't want to scare you."

As quickly as he blinked, she hurled herself at him. They fell back against the bed and she stared down at him, an odd look of pleasure and irritation on her face.

"Trust me, you're not going to scare me."

He cupped her cheeks, unable to help himself. He kissed her hard, telling her everything that words couldn't say. She was right there with him, touching and tasting.

"You have no idea just how badly I want you.

All the things I want to do with you. To you," he said against her throat. "But I'm barely in control and there's an animal inside me who won't be gentle with you, *cherié*."

His words halted her and after a moment, she rolled away.

"Do I get to tie you up later?" she asked, her humor shining through.

"I'll think about it," he said and reached for the rope. She didn't protest as he tied her wrists above her head. Somehow, he managed to ignore the lithe body, ripe with desire that beckoned to him. "Now, tell me about these dreams of yours. I want to hear every detail." He moved down the bed trailing his fingers over her leg, loving the way chill bumps broke out in his wake.

"Sebastian!"

"I told you, *cher*, no touching."

"I can't touch you with my legs."

He was sure that if there'd been more light, the look he gave her would have made her blush. He wrapped a piece of the rope around one ankle and then cinched it to the post on the footboard.

"Don't be shy, *chérie*. I've had dreams about you as well. Dreams where you ride my cock for hours."

His words must have excited her. She sighed low and long, and he could feel her pulse jump beneath his fingers as he tied her other ankle.

"I've probably dreamed about you every

night for a decade. Even when I shouldn't have. About what your skin would feel like against mine."

"I dreamt that too," she said.

He crawled up the length of her body, letting the hair on his chest tickle her. "How does it feel?" Slowly he nibbled his way down her jaw to her ear. She sighed and arched against him. God, she smelled good.

"Wonderful. Wonderful. Please Sebastian..."

"What is it, *amour*?"

"Touch me..."

"Where?" He laughed at her exasperated sigh.

He caressed her cheek with the back of her fingers. "Here?"

She shook her head.

"Here?" He cupped her breast and tugged on the nipple. She squirmed against him, her pelvis rubbing against his cock. He rolled to the side, at a safer distance.

"No!"

He moved his hand up to her collarbone. "How about—"

"No! Down there. For heaven's sakes. Don't make me beg! Touch me!" Her pleas made him laugh, as did her modesty. She'd quickly outgrow that.

Werewolves weren't known for their modesty. They had no problem with colorful language or nudity.

"Ahh... you want me to play with that pretty pussy. Is that it?"

She nodded enthusiastically.

"Say it," he whispered against her ear.

"Wh...what?" she stammered.

"I want to hear you say it."

"Oh, for heaven—"

He slid his palm down her tummy and let it rest right above the nest of curls between her legs. He could feel her straining to move underneath his hand.

"I'm not touching you until you say it."

"Touch my pussy, Sebastian." Her words were even, almost clinical, but it was her tone that told him how desperate she was. It was the rise and fall of her chest, the ragged breath against his cheek.

His fingers slid through her wet curls and between her delicate folds. She was so wet. So warm and just waiting for him. "Good girl. Now that wasn't hard was it?"

He circled her clit with the tip of his finger. Slow lazy circles that had her hips lifting off the bed.

"A little anxious, are we?"

"Sebastian!"

"Sorry love." He settled himself between her thighs and kissed every inch he could reach. The sweet scent of her swirled around him; filled him until he felt as if he were drowning in it. He sank a finger into her, coating it with her juices.

"Now, tell me about those dreams so I can make you come."

"We're in the woods. You're always chasing me," she offered so quickly it made him laugh.

"Do I catch you?"

He kissed and nipped his way up her thigh. Her legs spread wider and he lapped up her cream, loving the taste. Memorizing her musky scent. He turned his finger left and right and slowly curled it forward. Her hips shot off the bed and she cried out.

"Found it… Tell me more."

Her body tightened up, every tendon and muscle. He could see her pulling on the ropes, but he'd tied them carefully. They wouldn't come undone without his help.

"You catch me. You rip my clothes off and toss me to the ground."

He sucked on her clit just enough to make her gasp. Then he stopped and waited for her to continue.

"You thrust your fingers inside me, but I'm already wet. I'm always wet for you."

He groaned low in his throat. "I like the sound of that. How many fingers?"

"Two, sometimes three."

"Think you can take three fingers, *petite*?"

"I hope so."

He chuckled and asked her why. Before she

could answer, he added a digit turning them inside her slippery channel.

"Because you have a huge cock, that's why. Sebastian, *please*."

"What? What do you want?"

God, he sounded just like he had in her dreams. Amanda was about to come apart and he only had two fingers in her. The roar of the storm was nothing compared to the quake building deep inside her.

"Tell me, *chérie*. So, I can make you come." He went back to work scissoring his fingers and lapping at her pussy. Every so often, he hit her clit just right and she felt a spark of pleasure. She dug her heels into the bed as best she could, so she could drive herself against his fingers, his incredible mouth.

Just when she thought he might let her come, he pulled out his fingers and licked at her juices with his velvety tongue.

"Oh, God. Yes!"

He sampled her, nibbled on the tender flesh. She cried out when he slowly speared her with his tongue. Her cries turned to screams as he thrust faster and faster into her. Deeper. She had to have more.

Something bigger.

She was starting to feel dizzy. Starting to wonder if the orgasm would ever hit her. It was so close. So wonderfully close.

A bolt of lightning lit the room giving her a view of the handsome man between her thighs. She tossed her head back and pulled on the ropes again. This wasn't fair. She wanted to touch him. To feel him. She'd fantasized so many times about learning every inch of his body and now he was so close.

Then he stopped.

She whimpered. "Sebastian!"

"Relax, love." No sooner had the words left his lips than three thick fingers filled her. "Now, you were telling me about your dream. About my fingers pumping in and out of you. Like this?"

"Yes." She could barely find her voice when he was touching her like that.

"What next?"

"Please, Sebastian."

"Please what?"

"Untie me," she whined. "Enough is enough."

"I told you, no touching—"

Exasperated, she stared down at him, barely able to make out his face in the darkness. "I don't want to touch you. I want you to fuck me. Now."

He froze. For five whole heartbeats, he didn't move a single muscle and she started to wonder if she'd shocked him. Then in a lightning fast move, he was circling the bed, snapping the ropes.

"Ready for this, *petite*?" he asked, his voice dark and low.

"Yes!" Her cry was punctuated by a loud

crack of thunder. It was as if the heavens had been waiting for this very moment just as she had.

He crawled across the big bed and settled himself between her thighs. She ran her hands up over his arms, memorizing with her touch what her eyes couldn't see. He repositioned his hips and the broad tip of cock nestled against her opening.

He thrust himself home in one fluid motion. She screamed out in pleasure and pain. Neither of them moved for endless seconds. He kept his arms bracketed around her and she ran her hands down his sides, silently urging him to make love to her.

Finally, slowly he pulled back. For a moment, she felt empty but then he was inside her again, filling her. She angled her hips and he sank deeper. With each thrust, they found a rhythm. Him driving forward and her lifting her hips to meet him. He nuzzled her neck, his chest grazing her breasts with each movement.

She recognized the tender caress for what it was, a man barely holding onto his control. He pumped his cock into her faster and faster. She wrapped her legs around him, her moans growing louder.

She'd never felt this good before. This complete.

"Am I hurting you?" he asked when she moaned low in her throat.

"No. Harder. Faster."

She realized very quickly that human men were no match for werewolves. He fucked her harder *and* faster. So hard, she thought they'd break the bed. So fast, she could scarcely breathe. But her body accepted him. Welcomed the onslaught.

Then, as if she'd just leapt off a cliff into the turquoise waters of the ocean, she came. She moaned out her pleasure as it crashed into her like a tidal wave. Every cell in her body seemed energized and blissfully happy.

She heard the throaty grunts and groans of the man above her, her husband, who was thrusting for all he was worth.

With a loud shout of raunchy French, he froze inside her, his cock shooting his seed deep into her body. His muscles were hard beneath her fingertips, but they were also quivering. When he collapsed against her, she lazily ran her fingertips over his back.

"I love you," she whispered.

"I love you too, Amanda St. James." He rose up just enough to kiss her chin.

"Deveraux," she corrected.

"You're right. Mrs. Deveraux. Has a nice ring to it."

"It certainly does."

7

Darkness fell over the cabin and the winds eventually died down. Amanda had never felt so wonderful or so safe. They lay there, wrapped in each other's arms until sleep finally claimed them.

In the early hours of the morning, Amanda nestled against Sebastian's chest and her gaze swept the room, landing on her purse. She knew what the leather satchel contained. The letter from her father. The bastard. He'd barely acknowledged her while he was alive and yet he'd thought it a good idea to write her a letter before the cancer took him.

Surprisingly the bitterness she'd felt since she'd learned of his passing wasn't quite as strong as it had been. If anything, what she felt now was more akin to pity. For both of her parents really, they'd never been able to work out their differences and lead a full life.

Now that she and Sebastian were married, minus a few legalities with the American government, she was never going to let him go. She would fight for him and their relationship and they would communicate come hell or high water.

A clap of thunder shook the cabin, but she wasn't scared. As Sebastian had said, the structure was sturdy, state of the art even. The storm shutters were sealed tight and he'd informed her that the foundation layer of the house was nothing but a big barge. Should the waters get this high, they'd simply float.

"Why are you awake, *chérie*? Thought I wore you out." Sebastian's voice was wicked and seductively lazy.

"Just thinking."

"About?"

"My father." She'd stopped calling him dad a long time ago.

"He's dead, petite. He can't hurt you anymore."

Oh yes, he could. "He wrote me a letter." And she had a feeling that if she read it, he could torment her all over again.

Sebastian's sharp inhale told her all she needed to know about his thoughts on that subject. He'd been with her on some of her lowest days. He knew how much her father had hurt her with his yo-yoing ways. He'd seen the devastation on her mother's face. Even when she'd tried to hide the raw truth, he'd seen the ugly reality of her situation.

He'd never judged, only offered support and protection.

She realized now that he'd been torn up inside about their budding relationship and that's what had caused the wild mood shifts, the fighting between the brothers.

"Have you read it?"

She shook her head. Between the funeral and visiting with the lawyers she hadn't had the time or courage. Not that she thought it would take very long to read. The emotional recovery, that would take much longer.

He was finally dead. Outliving her mother by a decade. But from what she saw at the funeral, his life hadn't been happy or full. Stoic, staid, oppressive. Perhaps he'd done her a favor by never claiming her. Perhaps he'd saved her from a truly unhappy existence by not marrying her mom. But that was all ancient history and it belonged in the past.

"Do you want me to read it?" Sebastian asked.

She shrugged. This was the last thing, the final thread that connected her to her father. Now that he was dead, she never needed to think of him again. And if reading the letter meant cutting that tie and being done with it so she could finally, freely and completely move forward then that's what she needed to do.

Slipping from the bed, she didn't bother to hide her nudity. Her toes sank into the plush rug and then met the cool wood floor. She felt Sebastian's gaze warming her skin and took great pleasure in the ease she felt with him. They would know each other in all ways.

She pulled the envelope from her purse, picked up the lighter and another candle and then approached the bed. After handing him the letter she lit the candle and placed it on the bedside table.

The sheets were warm and soft as she sank down beside him. His long fingers plucked the letter from the envelope and unfolded it carefully. His dark gaze met hers for an instant before returning to the page.

For several long minutes he read silently, and his mouth got tighter and then softened.

"Do I want to know what it says?" she asked when she couldn't take the anticipation any longer.

He reorganized the pages and nodded. "*Oui.*"

He pushed up, so he was sitting against the headboard and then held out his arms, so she could snuggle against him. She stared at the perfectly defined muscles of his chest and was dumbfounded. That was the only word that made sense. He was so beautiful, so exquisitely formed. Not to mention warm and…hers. All hers.

She leaned forward and placed a kiss against his chest, right over his heart. Taking the letter, she settled against him, took a deep breath and began to read.

Dear Amanda,

I have many regrets in my life. You have never been one of them. I know I was a lousy dad and I wasn't good to your mom. She deserved better. You deserved better. You still do. You always will.

For the longest time I was angry. Angry at myself for not being stronger and angry at her for loving me. She wouldn't stop; couldn't stop I guess. And I would lose my temper and she would put herself in the firing line. I guess she thought she could save me, save us. But I wasn't strong enough to choose her over my family and expectations. I should have been. I see that now with perfect clarity that hindsight brings.

The doctor says the cancer is back and I should make my final arrangements. I don't have that many to make which is a sad state of things. I don't tell you this so you'll pity me. Let it be an example.

Live your life, Amanda. Not the life anyone else wants for you. Follow your heart and desires and don't let anyone else stand in your way. Be stronger than I was, more courageous. I knew from the time that you were little that you were smarter than me, more stubborn too.

Amanda laughed and wiped away a tear.

Don't grow old alone, surrounded by strangers. Build a family. Make close friendships that will last a lifetime. And whatever you do, don't have any regrets. Regrets at my age, with no time left to remedy them are almost as bad as hurting the ones you love.
Dad

She blew out a slow sigh and read the letter again.

"That's not what I expected."

"At least he admitted to his short-comings."

She nodded, feeling a little numb as she processed the words. Her father had been right about one thing. She didn't want to live with any regrets. She wanted a close family, a large family, children and friendships that would last a lifetime.

And she wanted Sebastian at her side.

———

WHEN AMANDA WOKE, light was just starting to come through the bedroom door. The spot next to her was empty. She sat up and looked around the room.

"Sebastian?"

"Out here, *chérie*."

She followed the sound of his voice and found him sitting in a lone chair on the deck, his gaze fixed on the light blue sky. The door was propped open and the shutters had been raised.

"Storm headed east so we didn't get the worst of it." He smiled up at her and she felt her insides turn to mush all over again.

The black robe didn't look nearly as big on him as it had on her. She bent to give him a kiss and he pulled her onto his lap. His strong arms wrapped around her naked body, holding her close.

"I will never get tired of kissing you," he informed her.

She laughed and wrapped her arms around his neck. As she gazed into his dark eyes, she wondered why she'd ever stayed away.

"You must stay, you know. You're to be my Luna now."

"Your Luna?"

"My mate. The leader of our pack. You're the Alpha female now."

"Does that mean that you have to do whatever I tell you?" she teased and trailed her fingers down the hard plain of his chest.

"I might let you have your way every now and then," he said and cupped her left breast in his hand. She arched against him and felt the hard ridge between them.

"Sebastian!" she said, shocked at his eagerness. "You're hard again."

"I cannot help it, *cherié*. It's your fault. It's what being near you does to me."

It was time for some payback.

"Is that right?" She tugged at the ties holding the robe closed and let them fall away. She stared deep into his eyes as she brushed the soft fabric away from his body. Bracing her hands against his chest, she straddled his hips and slowly drank in the sight of him sans clothing.

Hot was an understatement. No wonder he was the most eligible bachelor in Louisiana.

Not anymore. A smile spread across her face and she began to rub against the hard length of him.

He sucked in a breath and looked at her through his lashes. "What are you smiling about, love?"

"You're not the most eligible—bachelor—in Louisiana—anymore," she said, concentrating of the friction between her legs.

Her juices covered his cock, making for a slippery ride. He bucked his hips and almost succeeded in sliding home. She pushed him down and shook her head.

"It's my turn to drive you wild."

"You do that every day." His hands closed around her hips and he pushed his hips up against hers.

She was rapidly losing control of both her desire and him, and the look in his dark eyes said he knew it. He reached between her legs and flicked the sensitive nub.

Quickly, she stood up and turned around. "You're not getting your way," she told him over her shoulder.

He growled low in his throat, but the sound didn't scare her. She reached beneath her and guided his cock into her wet sheath.

Bracing her hands against his thighs, she began moving up and down on his cock. She kept the rhythm tortuously slow. He was so big, so thick. His hands raked over her back and she fought the urge to lean back against him, to let him take the lead.

His arm snaked around her waist and his fingers closed over her clit, making her cry out.

"I should tie you up since you can't keep your hands to yourself."

"Not a chance in hell." The possessive tone set off something inside her. She tossed her head back and rode him as hard as she could. An orgasm swept over her, heating her from the inside out, shocking her with its quickness.

She was almost embarrassed, but he kept his fingers pressed firmly against her. She moaned long and low and slowed to a stop.

"We're not done, beautiful," he whispered into her ear.

In the blink of an eye, he'd pushed them out of the chair and bent her over the railing, his cock still balls deep inside her. He brushed her hair to the side and rained kisses over her back and shoulders.

She braced her hands against the wet wood and stared down into the dark waters. Her breasts dangled into space and she suddenly wondered if anyone could see them. She looked out at the quiet landscape and pastel sunrise.

"No one can see you, *chérie*. We're out here all alone." He nipped her shoulder blade with his teeth. An excited shiver raced over her skin and she pushed back against his cock. He pulled all the way out and then thrust into her. "No one to hear you scream."

His words brought another flood of desire, of moisture. Clamping his hands over her hips, he started a slow motion, almost a twist as he pushed himself inside her heat. Cries of delight erupted from her throat and carried over the water.

Faster and faster he moved, his hot breath panting against her neck.

"Come for me," he whispered and rubbed her clit.

"You first," she replied, squeezing his cock with her muscles. A deep sound, almost a roar, burst from his throat. He swelled inside her and came with force. At the same moment, sharp teeth clamped over the base of her neck causing her to scream. Tears stung her eyes, but the pain was quickly replaced by pleasure. He pressed against her clit and she came again, crying out his name. Her knees went weak, and she was glad she was trapped between the solidness of Sebastian and the strong wooden railing. She was utterly spent.

"I love you," he said, his voice thick with emotion. He kissed the tender spot on the back of her neck.

Love and pleasure wrapped her like a blanket. Moisture slicked her thighs, but she didn't care. She had Sebastian. Finally. After all the yearning and waiting, she had his love.

She was home.

This isn't the end…

It's only the beginning. Keep reading for a sneak peek of Bitten In the Bayou, Jules' story.

When wildlife photographer Angelica Humphries woke up this morning, she never expected to end up in a cabin with two sexy Cajuns. Wild birds are more her speed. But when a powerful hurricane threatens, she'd be crazy not to take them up on their offer of shelter and protection. Right?

Jules and Andre Deveraux were hired to find Angelica, not fall for her. Tracking her through the bayou was the easy part. Keeping the secret that would ruin any chance Jules has with the strawberry blonde beauty, so much harder. But he'll do whatever it takes, because one sniff and he knows she's meant to be his.

. . .

WARNING: Contains two sinfully handsome Cajun werewolves with voracious appetites, a splash of danger and a naughty game of scrabble.

THE SUN BROKE through the dark thundercloud and warmed the damp earth. Jules Deveraux turned to his brother André and frowned. "See anything?"

André shook his dark head. "*Non.*"

They'd been in town for supplies, waiting for the latest hurricane to blow to shore when a distressed businessman had stormed in looking for his missing girlfriend. He'd hired André and Jules to find her, to bring her back safely. No one knew the swamp and the forest as well as the Deveraux brothers.

So here they were. On the chase. Not that Jules minded. He was a wolf in human clothing after all.

As quick as the sun had come, it went. Thunder rumbled in the distance, and the wind picked up again. The scent of muck and rain swirled around him. He sniffed the air for any scent of the woman.

"He must love her an awful lot, *non*? To come here looking for her?"

"His concern seemed... genuine," André said, leaning down to study a patch of earth.

This would go a lot faster if they were in wolf form, but they couldn't risk being seen. The storm chasers and weather reporters were already setting up shop, waiting for the next big one. Jules had seen enough storms to have a good idea which ones would pass them by. Perhaps it was just a sixth sense.

"You don't sound as if you believe that, *mon frere*," he said as they pushed their way farther into the forest.

"I don't."

"Neither do I. He seemed *too* concerned."

"Too possessive," André agreed.

Jules caught the scent of lilac and inhaled appreciatively. Warm, distinctly floral with a hint of woman. He'd found her.

"Come on." He took off jogging.

Lightning crackled overhead, charging the air with its energy. They had to find her and get the hell outta here, fast. If there was one thing Jules knew, it was that lightning, tall trees and water don't mix. He paused and caught her scent again. He turned right and pushed the low hanging limbs out of the way.

The boom of thunder told him the storm was getting close. He saw something through the leaves. Something pink. He motioned for his brother to look in that direction. André nodded, his gaze fixed on the spot.

There she was.

The scent grew stronger, surrounding them. Swirling on the wind. Intoxicating him. She smelled... ripe. Delicious. Unexpected... but familiar.

Odd. He was sure they'd never met before.

Together they stepped forward, silently, until they had a better view.

Angelica Humphrey's picture hadn't done her justice. Her golden hair was captured loosely at her neck. Several tendrils escaped, cascading around her face. She looked through the view finder of a camera, completely oblivious to their presence.

Didn't she know there were predators about?

André must have sensed his thoughts. A tight smile curved his lips upward, and they shared a glance.

Her petal pink t-shirt was peppered with raindrops. It outlined her lush breasts and trim waist. A sage green rain slicker was cinched around her hips and her form-fitting jeans flared at the bottom over a pair of boots that had seen better days. A dingy camera bag sat at her feet.

Angelica felt a zing along the back of her neck. That same zing had often warned her of danger or where to be to get the best shot possible. It had warned her away from William, thank God. Despite his Golden Child good looks, he was a dark and dangerous man. Possessive and ruthless.

Slowly she lowered her camera till it dangled from her neck. The snap of a twig made her look right. Two men stepped out of the trees and into the clearing.

Her first instinct was to run.

But for some reason she stayed put, looking them over. The one on the left was tall, trim, with unruly black hair. He had sharply chiseled features. Some might even call him beautiful. But his lean frame proclaimed he was all man.

"Angelica Humphrey?" the other man asked.

He was only an inch or so shorter and far more rugged. Muscles shimmered beneath his T-shirt. He had the same dark hair, unreadable eyes, and rosy lips.

A coil of desire tightened low in her belly, surprising her. She hadn't felt honest to goodness desire in a very long time.

"How do you know my name?" she asked, mentally calculating how fast she could pull the knife from her boot. She never traveled without protection. As a wildlife photographer she sometimes came across beasts that needed taming.

"William Bardsley asked us to find you. I'm André Deveraux, and des is my brother Jules." His accent was delicious and wicked. His brother gave her a friendly smile, one that was supposed to put her at ease, no doubt. But it just made all her muscles tighten.

William had sent them?

They didn't look like William's thugs. She'd never warmed to any of his friends or... associates.

"You don't look like you need finding," the taller one, Jules, murmured. A dark eyebrow inched up slightly as he took in her raincoat and boots.

"Why don't you run along and tell William that I meant it when I said it was over."

The two men shared a glance. Jules put his hand on his hips. The rain picked up again, and she quickly shrugged into her coat.

"He's not your boyfriend?" Jules asked. An unreadable expression crossed his face.

Angelica couldn't stop the laugh that erupted from her lips. "Hardly. We were dating. I said it was over. William's the type that always gets what he wants. No matter the cost to anyone else."

She bent to put her camera in her bag, making sure to keep an eye on them. Overhead, the wind howled through the trees and the birds she'd been photographing took flight. "Better yet, don't tell him you found me at all."

Slowly she backed away from them.

"If he's not your boyfriend, why did he come all this way to find you?"

That had her stopping in her tracks. A trickle of fear tiptoed up her spine.

"He came here?"

André nodded.

"We met him in town. What in the world are

you doin' out here anyway? Don't you know there's a hurricane a comin?" Jules asked.

Angelica nodded. She did indeed know there was a hurricane coming. "That's why I'm here. I'm a wildlife photographer."

"A wildlife photographer?" André asked, as if he'd never heard of the concept before. He stepped closer, and Angelica's heartbeat picked up speed. Didn't they care that they were getting soaked? Their T-shirts seemed to be melting against their tanned skin. Another clap of thunder shook the ground, jolting her nerves.

Jules spoke quietly to André in what sounded like French. His voice was rich like Swiss chocolate. André nodded, and they both settled their gazes upon her. Tingles erupted over her skin, her breasts tightened and the trickle of desire exploded into full blown need.

"I, ugh, I've gotta go. Nice meeting you." She turned like a scared deer and ran.

She'd gotten all of three feet before a strong hand clamped down on her wrist and spun her around. A scream froze in throat when she found herself pinned to Jules' tall frame.

"Not that way. Wanna get eaten by a gator?"

Again that dark eyebrow mocked her. But she couldn't find the energy to care. She was too aware of the flat planes of his stomach, his rock hard thigh between hers, the corded muscles beneath her fingertips. Her breath stalled in her lungs as she looked way up, her gaze meeting his.

He'd asked her a question. Silently, she shook her head. No, she didn't want to get eaten by an alligator. But she wondered what it would be like to be gobbled up by a sexy Cajun.

She stomped down on that thought. If William had come after her, he was more serious than she'd originally thought. She needed to disappear for a while. Good thing she'd brought her passport.

"What do they call this color, André?" Jules' unexpected question confused her. His eyes flicked over the top of her head.

"Strawberry blonde?" the other man replied. He sounded like he was right behind her. She turned her head and saw him out of the corner of her eye. Only a foot or so separated her back from his front. She'd be lying if she said their nearness didn't affect her. Excite her just a little.

She'd traveled the world, and though she'd always had her lens zoomed in on animals, she'd kept an eye out for Mr. Right. Or Mr. Hot-n-Sexy. She'd never come across a man so worthy of being photographed. A man so gorgeous he could steal her breath. One who had an animal magnetism that was usually reserved for movie stars.

Until now.

And there were two of them, she thought,

feeling rather dreamy despite the fact that she was sinking into the mud.

"Right," Jules murmured, drawing her attention back to him. "Strawberry blonde. I love strawberries, don't you André?"

His tone was so seductive, so husky, Angelica's insides melted. Her hardened nipples brushed against his chest, and she knew she should back away from him. Get as far away from these men as she could.

"Mmm, hmm."

"So juicy. And sweet," Jules whispered in her ear. A little thrill raced through her as his breath warm caressed her wet skin. When he straightened and actually licked his lips, she was sure he was going to kiss her.

Angelica found strength she didn't know she had and took a step back. Self-preservation. She had to get out of this swamp. Away from William. No matter how seductive these men were.

Her back hit something strong and solid. Not a tree. André.

Large hands clamped over her hips, and a squeak of alarm escaped her lips.

"What's wrong, *chérie*?" Jules stepped toward her, his hands capturing hers. He breathed on them, letting his hot breath chase away the chill.

"No—nothing." She shook her head. When he looked up at her through those long, black eyelashes, Angelica realized she was a goner.

They'd completely and utterly seduced her with their heated looks, sexy accent, and tender touch. "Is William still in town?" she found herself asking.

Jules tensed for just a second before he shrugged those strong shoulders. "Dunno."

"Does it matter?" André asked.

"He's a dangerous man." Her voice shook more than she wanted.

Jules' jaw worked back and forth, and his hazel eyes darkened to match the stormy sky. "Don't worry, *chérie*. We'll protect you."

Get your copy at: http://selena-blake.com/bitb

A NOTE FROM SEBASTIAN

Wondering about the flowers? Me too. Keep reading the Stormy Weather series to learn all our secrets. The next book in the series, *Bitten in the Bayou*, follows my brother Jules into the heart of Louisiana.

A NOTE FROM THE AUTHOR

Dear Reader,

I hope you enjoyed Amanda and Sebastian's love story. I love a happily ever after, don't you? The good news is, this is only the beginning. There are more books in the Stormy Weather series, giving you the chance to see more of Manda and Sebastian. It's going to be a stormy few months in the bayou.

Since I know you don't want to miss any upcoming book news I keep my website updated regularly and you can frequently find me chatting with readers on my blog.

And if you're in the market for free books, be sure to sign up for my newsletter. Joining gets you instant access to my Members Only lounge and every good WolfCub knows that the Members Only Lounge is where it's at. That exclusive key gets you into the Wolfpack. And there are currently free reads waiting for you. Ready to sign up? http://selena-blake.com/members/

I hope you enjoyed The Cajun Werewolf's Captive. But even if you didn't, I'd still appreciate a review. I read each and every one and I learn from them so that each book is better than the last. If you're not sure where to leave a review, here are a few suggestions. Why not start at the site where you purchased your copy? I'm active on Goodreads and review books there myself. Look me up. There's also BookBub. If you have a blog, that'd be a great place too.

As always, I love hearing from my readers. You can write to me at Selena@selena-blake.com.

Happy Reading,

Selena

ABOUT THE AUTHOR

An action movie buff with a penchant for all things supernatural and sexy, Selena Blake combines her love for adventure, travel and romance into steamy paranormal romance. Selena's books have been called "a steamy escape" and have appeared on bestseller lists, been nominated for awards, and won contests. When she's not writing you can find her by the pool soaking up some sun, day dreaming about new characters, and watching the cabana boy (aka her muse), Derek. Fan mail keeps her going when the diet soda wears off so write to her at selenablake@gmail.com.

Newsletter:
http://www.selena-blake.com/members/

Stay In Touch
selena-blake.com
selena@selena-blake.com

- facebook.com/SelenaBlakeFanClub
- twitter.com/selenablake
- instagram.com/selenaablake

OTHER BOOKS BY SELENA BLAKE

Series: Paranormal Protectors: New Orleans
Bewitched by His Fated Mate
Claiming His Forbidden Witch
Resisting the Vampire's Kiss

Series: Stormy Weather
The Cajun Werewolf's Captive
Bitten in the Bayou
Seduced by a Cajun Werewolf
Mated to a Cajun Werewolf
Stranded with a Cajun Werewolf
A Cajun Werewolf Christmas

Series: Mystic Isle
Fangs, Fur & Forever
A Werewolf to Call Her Own
Games Demons Play
Pursued by a Werewolf
Bound to the Vampire

Short Stories

Kissing Wilde

Anthologies

Stormy Weather Collector's Edition (5-in-1, plus interviews, deleted scenes and more)

Mystic Isle

Single Titles

Ready & Willing - There can be only one alpha.

―――

Selena writes contemporary romance and romantic suspense under the name Gillian Blakely.

Printed in Great Britain
by Amazon